Death Down Under

Roy MacGregor

D1317041

M&S

An M&S Paperback Original from
McClelland & Stewart Ltd.
The Canadian Publishers

For Jesse and Justin Barnett, the California Owls

The author is grateful to Doug Gibson, who thought up this series, and to Alex Schultz, who pulls it off.

National Library of Canada Cataloguing in Publication Data

MacGregor, Roy, 1948–
   Death down under

(The Screech Owls series; 15)
ISBN 0-7710-5644-3

I. Title.   II. Series: MacGregor, Roy, 1948– .
Screech Owls series; 15.

PS8575.G84D42 2001   jC813'.54   C2001-930732-2
PZ7.M334De 2001

We acknowledge the financial support of the Government of Canada through the Book Publishing Industry Development Program for our publishing activities.

Cover illustration by Gregory C. Banning
Typeset in Bembo by M&S, Toronto

Printed and bound in Canada

McClelland & Stewart Ltd.
The Canadian Publishers
481 University Avenue
Toronto, Ontario
M5G 2E9
www.mcclelland.com

1 2 3 4 5   05 04 03 02 01

"IS IT STILL FLUSHING BACKWARDS?"

"*Drop dead!*"

The first voice belonged to Fahd; the second, coming from inside the toilet bowl, belonged to Nish. The first was laughing, and the second sounded, understandably, near tears.

Nish was throwing up in the bathroom. Not *pretend* hurling for once, but really being sick.

Travis felt like he might be next. A few minutes earlier he had even scurried into the little hotel bathroom himself, the same bathroom where most of the Screech Owls had gathered earlier in the day while Nish – using the vitamin pills his mother always packed – had given a demonstration how toilets here flushed in the opposite direction.

"Only Nish would know which way they go down back home," sneered Sarah, who'd come in with Sam to watch.

It had been hilarious, with Nish red-faced and grunting as he climbed up on the sink and reached over to let the little brown pills plop loudly into the toilet bowl before he pressed the flush lever with his toes to send them swirling in what he explained was the reverse of normal, clockwise rather than counter-clockwise, down, down through the hotel waste system.

But no one was laughing now. Travis had been sure he, too, would be sick to his stomach, but all he could do was retch a couple of times and wish, more than anything else in the world, that Nish had been right.

That everything here did run backwards.

Including time.

Travis's stomach hurt. His temples hurt. The back of his neck hurt like he'd been cross-checked headfirst into the boards.

And yet the Owls still hadn't played a single hockey game in Australia. They'd been so excited about that first game Down Under, but now it was impossible even to think about playing hockey. Who could, after what had happened?

The team had never been so up for a trip. They had visited some exciting places before, but this trip was special, because it had come to them completely out of the blue and involved probably the last place on earth any of them ever thought they'd be playing their favourite game.

It all began with a letter that had arrived one

day in the downtown office of Mr. Lindsay, Travis's father:

The Australian Ice Hockey Federation, in an effort to promote minor hockey development in Australia, would like to extend an invitation to the Tamarack Screech Owls to come to Sydney, Australia, for the first-ever "Oz Peewee Invitational."

The trip would coincide almost exactly with the March school break.

Travis's father had been surprised there was even ice in Australia, let alone a national ice hockey organization. Australia, Mr. Lindsay said, was probably the top sporting country in the world, but the sports they played were soccer and cricket and swimming and track-and-field and basketball. When a country was mostly desert, when the temperature on a bright January day could reach forty-eight degrees Celsius, well on the way to making ice *boil*, hockey was hardly the game that came to mind.

But Mr. Lindsay, as president of the Tamarack Minor Hockey Association, discovered that little in Australia is ever quite what it first seems. The Australians would pick up all costs, including airfare, for the Screech Owls peewee hockey team and their coach and manager. All that was requested in return was that in the future the

Screech Owls invite an Australian team to take part in a minor hockey tournament put on by the town of Tamarack.

But there was more. The Australians were convinced they could not really compete against the Screech Owls in the "Oz Invitational," and so the games would be exhibition only. To add to the competitive edge, however, the City of Sydney would put on a "Mini-Olympics" at the same time, to be held at many of the same facilities that had been used for the Sydney Summer Olympics – the best Summer Games ever, many people thought.

"Can I do synchronized swimming?" Nish had asked when Muck read the letter to them in the Owls dressing room after practice.

"Better that than beach volleyball!" Sam had shouted from the other end of the room. "At least that big butt of yours would be under water."

"Imagine Nish in a *thong*!" Sarah had laughed, kicking off her skates.

"People have seen me in less," Nish shot back, his face reddening as he leaned over to loosen his laces.

"Don't remind me," Travis said, wincing at the flood of memories: Nish in the Swedish sauna, Nish and the World's Biggest Skinny Dip at summer hockey camp, Nish running nude on Vancouver's Wreck Beach, Nish planning to "moon" the entire world at Times Square . . .

From the moment Muck read that letter, the excitement had built. They were going to the land of kangaroos, koalas, platypus, crocodiles, and the deadly Great White Shark. They were going to Sydney, that magnificent city they'd all seen on television during the Olympics Games. And they were going to be in their own Mini-Olympics.

Dmitri was talking about running the 100-metre dash. Travis wanted to try the mountain bike course. Liz, who was on a swim team, couldn't believe she'd be getting a chance to try out the Olympic pool. Wilson, probably the Owls' strongest player, wanted to try weightlifting. Little Simon Milliken said he knew how to wrestle. Derek and Jesse wanted to form a team for tennis doubles. Sarah and Sam said they were going to be the Owls' official beach volleyball team, and Sarah, the team's best athlete, also wanted to enter all the races and swimming events.

"Rhythmic gymnastics," Nish had said one day at practice. "I think *that's* my new sport. You know, prancing about and throwing a ribbon up in the air and catching it."

"Get serious," Travis had told him.

"I'm also thinking about synchronized diving," Nish said, leaning back in his stall, his eyes closed dreamily.

"What?" Sam had yelled over. "You and a *boulder*!"

"Nah. Me 'n' you – how about it?"

Nish had meant it as a joke. With his eyes still closed, he hadn't seen Sam winking at Sarah.

"You're on, Big Boy – me 'n' you!"

Nish's eyes had popped open, but it was too late. The whole team loved the idea.

Sam was an excellent diver. There wasn't a player on the team who didn't remember her wild leap from the rocks high over the Ottawa River when they'd gone rafting. But neither was there an Owl who didn't know that Wayne Nishikawa, the World's Biggest Big Talker, was terrified, absolutely petrified, of heights.

Travis had smiled to himself. This was going to be interesting.

In the days that followed, Sarah Cuthbertson, more than any of the other Owls, had become consumed with the upcoming trip. She'd often said her greatest dream was to become a marine biologist, and she told them that Australia was like a dream come true. It was where the Great Barrier Reef was, and its waters offered the finest scuba diving and snorkelling in the world.

"I plan to see lots of seahorses, *and* my first Great White Shark," she said.

It would happen quicker than any of them imagined.

2

IT HAD TAKEN TWENTY-TWO HOURS TO FLY TO Australia, and after they'd been driven to the little hotel they'd be staying in down by Sydney's famous Opera House and Nish had given his ridiculous demonstration of the way toilets flush "backwards" in Australia, the Screech Owls had set out to shake off the jet lag with a quick tour of the harbour and the famous Sydney Aquarium.

A little green-and-yellow-and-red ferry boat – Travis was convinced it was identical to one he'd played with in the tub when he was much younger – had taken them out on a cruise around the magnificent, fin-shaped Opera House and then under the massive Sydney Harbour Bridge. It was a beautiful day, the water almost as blue as the clear sky.

Their guide, Mr. Spears, had pointed way up above the water to the highest spans of the bridge, where it seemed ants were moving along slowly. But they weren't ants – they were *people*. People climbing high over the top span of the enormous bridge.

"We call 'er 'The Coathanger,' mates," Mr. Spears had announced in his strong Australian accent. "Greatest view in all of Oz from up there."

Travis smiled. He liked the way Australians called their country "Oz." They said it with such affection. Travis couldn't think of a nickname that would work for Canada. "Can" sounded, well, *stupid*. People would think you were talking about a toilet, not a country.

"You have to tie ropes around your middle to go up," Mr. Spears told them. "And they charge a good fee – but it's well worth it, mates, well worth it. You should consider it while you're here."

"*No way!*" Nish had shouted.

"We could practise our synchronized dives from there," suggested Sam.

"Practise yourself! I'm not climbing anywhere except outta this stupid boat."

Travis had looked at his old friend. Nish was a bit green. The jet lag, the rolling of the ferry, the sight of people climbing high over the water – it was all a bit much for Nish's sensitive stomach. It was the only part of his friend, Travis thought, that had ever shown any sensitivity at all.

Soon, the bridge was well behind them and the ferry had dropped them off at Darling Harbour. They walked up along the wharf to the massive glass building that housed what Data claimed was the best aquarium anywhere.

"The Sydney Aquarium has saltwater crocodiles," Data said. "Grow more than twenty feet long and will attack and eat an entire cow – or a person, if they feel like it. Most dangerous animal on earth, I think."

"I thought the Great White Shark was," said Fahd.

"Earth, Fahd," corrected Data. "I said *earth* – sharks don't walk on land, do they?"

"Actually," Sarah said, interrupting, "you're both wrong. The truly scary creatures of Australia you wouldn't even notice."

"*Sure*," Nish said sarcastically. "Like what? Killer hamsters? Vampire goldfish? Sabre-toothed bunny rabbits?"

Sarah was smiling slightly. Travis noticed it even if Nish hadn't. He knew that Sarah had Nish right where she wanted him.

"Ever hear of the Box Jellyfish?" she asked.

"*Jell-O* fish?" Nish howled. "You gotta be kidding."

"Jell-*EEE* fish, dummy, and I'm not kidding," said Sarah. "You swim up against one of them and, if you live, you'll wish you hadn't. It's kind of like being skinned alive and then spray-painted with acid, they say."

"No way I'm even going swimming!" shouted Lars.

"There's none in the waters around Sydney," said Sarah.

9

"Good!" said Lars. "There better not be."

"In Sydney you have to watch out for the funnel web spider," Sarah said, her little smile returning. She was enjoying herself. "It's the most poisonous spider in the world."

"Will it kill you?" Fahd asked.

"Yes," said Sarah, "but slowly. First you bounce off the walls for a few hours like you're about to explode, then you start shaking, turn blue and shiver until you pass out. If they don't get the antidote into you in time, you're history."

Travis winced. Australia had seemed like such a warm and welcoming country, a bit like Canada, and a bit like the United States, and a bit like England, and a whole lot like itself. The last thing it seemed was dangerous. But now he wasn't so sure.

They had a wonderful tour of the aquarium. They all stood with their noses to the glass as harbour seals swam in dazzling circles only inches away. They saw the fearsome saltwater crocodiles in the "Rivers of the Far North" display. They spent more than an hour at the "Touch Pool," picking up hermit crabs and elephant snails and nervously handing around a shark-egg case as if it might suddenly split open to reveal a miniature "Jaws."

At the Great Barrier Reef display, Sarah found her beloved seahorses. There was a special exhibit of orange Big-belly Seahorses, hundreds of the oddly elegant creatures hovering about in a glass tank. Travis stared in wonder, baffled as to how a small bony fish could look so like a real horse, the arch of the neck and the head almost identical, the big yellow eyes filled with an intelligence and concentration that seemed impossible for such a tiny little thing. Travis felt as if *he* were on display and the seahorses examining him.

He could see how they'd managed to captivate Sarah, even if certain others could not.

"What's so special about these things?" Nish asked, unimpressed.

"They're an inspiration for women," said Sarah, turning her head slightly away as that mysterious smile danced again across her lips.

Nish's face twisted into a question: "What's *that* supposed to mean?"

"What do you know about seahorses, anyway?" Sarah asked.

"That you can't ride them?" Nish answered sarcastically. "That it's tough to find little saddles for them? How the heck should I know anything about them?"

"The males have the babies," said Sarah, winking over the tank at Sam, who was giggling.

"I'm not *stupid*!" Nish shouted.

"Can we vote on that?" Sam called over.

"MEN CAN'T HAVE BABIES," Nish insisted, all but stamping his feet.

"These men do," said Sarah. "The female gives him the eggs to carry, he fertilizes them and carries them in a pouch on his belly and later gives birth to them."

Nish's face was beet-red. "*I'm gonna hurl!*"

"Some of us like the idea," said Sarah.

"Maybe *you* could do it, Nish!" called out Sam. "You've already got the gut for it!"

Nish was trying to answer back. He stammered. He spat. He turned even redder. Then he stomped off, the laughter of the rest of the Owls ringing in his scarlet ears.

Travis felt sorry for his old friend. The girls had been a bit unfair. It wasn't Nish's fault he didn't know about seahorses. It wasn't his fault he was heavy. Travis would even have come to his rescue if Nish didn't always make fun of everyone else's shortcomings.

Saving the best for last, they wandered finally into the huge Oceanarium, a fascinating, twisting series of glassed-in tunnels through the water, where eels, stingrays, sea turtles, a dozen different varieties of fish, and even several sharks swam around them so close that the Owls felt the huge creatures might brush against them – or *bite*!

"We have a special treat for you, mates," said Mr. Spears after a quick discussion with one of the aquarium staff.

"What's that?" asked Fahd. All the Screech Owls were pressing in towards Mr. Spears and the attendant.

The attendant cleared her throat and spoke. "You're about to go through a tank holding a Great White Shark!"

"*NOOOO!*" screamed Sarah.

"*YESSSS!*" screamed Sam, meaning exactly the same thing.

"Yesterday, fishermen off the south coast had a Great White get tangled up in their nets. He was cut loose and placed in a transportation pool, and we've just released him into a special compartment here. No one else has seen him yet. You'll be first."

"*ALL RIGHT!*" the Screech Owls yelled together.

"You'll have to be quiet, though. He's not used to the tanks and he's never seen a group come through before. No tapping on the glass. No sudden movements. Promise?"

"*WE PROMISE!*" the Owls shouted.

Keeping very quiet, they moved into a tunnel that Travis had earlier noticed was blocked off from the public. The barriers were down now, and the lights were on, sending an eerie glow into the glass tunnels ahead of them. It was almost as if they were walking in outer space.

They came into a huge tank where, for the first time, there were no eels or turtles or fish of any kind sliding along the glass. This pool seemed empty, except for a large shadow at the far end.

The shadow moved!

Travis felt the entire group suck in its breath and hold it. It was as if they were suddenly *in* the water, not passing through in air tunnels. No one moved. No one spoke. No one even drew breath.

The Great White turned, its dark back as huge as a boat. It rolled slightly, white belly flashing.

Still no one dared breathe.

It drifted silently across the roof of the tunnel. Then it rolled again, one beady eye scanning the group as if it might be looking for an appetizer before settling down to a main course of peewee hockey team.

It made several passes over them, each time twisting slightly to stare.

Whenever it went by, it was as if a dark cloud were moving overhead. Travis could not believe its size. It was massive.

Its mouth opened slightly, revealing dozens of long, sword-sharp teeth.

"Toss him a Clorets!" snorted Nish.

The attendant immediately hushed him. No one laughed. Even Muck seemed awestruck, his own mouth wide as he stared up.

The shark's huge mouth opened again, bubbles rolling out.

"He's *burping*!" hissed Fahd.

This time someone did laugh: Nish, of course.

The Great White opened wider, and a flush of red-and-white shreds came out.

Travis could hear a quick intake of air as everyone gasped a second time.

What is it? wondered Travis. *Fish guts? Or maybe seal?*

The shark turned and passed again, dropping so low its fins touched the top of the tunnel. Travis could hear them rubbing, almost squeaking, against the glass.

The mouth opened again, and a great burst of bubbles rolled out and raced for the surface.

"Indigestion, pal?" whispered Nish.

The mouth opened even wider, and something else came out.

It was round and very white, trailing something dark, like string.

Travis tried to see as it thumped hard on the glass above their heads, then rolled off the tunnel roof through the churning, bubbling water.

He took a step closer, staring hard.

Not string – *more like hair!*

Black hair.

Down, down the object tumbled. It landed against a rock, bounced gently, then settled back, caught between the rock and an outcrop of coral.

The Screech Owls rushed over, then stopped abruptly.

It was a human head, partially digested – one milky eye staring up at them, the other socket empty.

Travis heard a loud thud behind him.

The attendant had fainted.

3

NISH WAS STILL THROWING UP IN THE BATH-room. Fahd was staring blankly at the TV while he flicked through the channels without stop-ping. Lars was asleep, tossing and twisting under the covers and groaning every now and then as if caught in a nightmare.

Travis was lying on his bed, pressing the tips of his fingers to his throbbing temples and wishing he could just stay there until the last five or six hours somehow magically erased themselves.

There was a light rap on the door. Fahd put down the remote and stood on his tiptoes to see out the peephole.

"It's Sarah," he said. "And Jenny and Sam and Liz."

"Let 'em in," Travis said. The girls were sharing the room next door. Perhaps they'd even heard Nish retching.

Before they could say anything, there came one huge retch from the bathroom, followed by Nish coughing and choking and spitting, then the flush of the toilet and the tap turning on, hard.

They waited, no one saying a word. Fahd began flicking mindlessly once more through the channels, but no one complained and no one asked him to stop. They all stared at the flickering screen, grateful for any distraction.

The door to the bathroom opened, and Nish, a bath towel wrapped around his head, stumbled out and promptly bumped into Sam, who was sitting on the edge of the bed.

The towel unwound to reveal a shining, pink face, eyes swollen and bloodshot, black hair soaking wet. Nish must have had his head right under the tap.

"Feel better, Barf Boy?" Sam asked.

Nish flicked the towel in her direction, snapping it harmlessly in the air.

"Something I ate," he mumbled. "Food poisoning, I guess."

Sarah couldn't help laughing. "Whoever got food poisoning from chocolate bars and Coke?"

"I eat other stuff!" Nish protested.

"No one's ever seen you!" Sarah said, giggling.

"How're you guys doing?" Travis asked.

"Not good," admitted Liz. "I can't get it out of my head."

"Neither can I," said Lars, now wide awake and disentangling himself from his sweat-soaked sheets.

The telephone rang, and Lars, who was closest, picked it up.

"Hello?" Lars said uncertainly. He nodded several times. Then said, "Okay," and hung up the receiver.

The others stared, waiting.

"It was Mr. Dillinger," Lars explained. "Muck's lined up a game for us. We're on the ice in an hour."

"*In an hour!*" Sam shouted, as if it were impossible.

But in a flash everyone was in action – Lars stabbing his feet into his shoes, even Nish diving into the heap in the corner that passed for his luggage to pull out a clean T-shirt and extra socks. They weren't tired. They'd slept most of the flight and, besides, the events of the past few hours had made relaxation impossible.

Muck was doing exactly the right thing, Travis realized. He was forcing them back into the world they knew best.

The Owls needed ice time.

4

TRAVIS KNEW HIS COMFORT ZONE. IT SMELLED of concrete and industrial cleaner and hot dogs rolling endlessly on a stainless steel grill. It sounded like a sharpening stone running dryly across a skate blade. Like the laughter of a dressing room, and the strange silence of a rink when the Zamboni has just finished. It was the sight of shining new ice just waiting for Travis Lindsay's skate blades to draw his favourite designs over it.

And Muck Munro knew it, too. He knew what the Screech Owls liked better than anything else in the world: a game where they could *play* – a game where the stands were empty and everyone could relax and enjoy the game they loved. It was just what they needed.

"We're playing the local rep team," Muck said. "Some of them are new to hockey, and they've never played a North American team before, so go easy on them and just have some fun. Don't even think of this as a practice. It's shinny – understand?"

Travis nodded. As captain, he had to understand a little better than the rest; it would be his job to make sure the shinny game went the way Muck wanted it to. That meant not embarrassing anyone, not running up the score if they had a chance, no rough stuff, certainly no fights, and no mouthing off.

In other words, it was Travis Lindsay's job to make sure Wayne Nishikawa was kept in line.

Travis leaned over and checked out Nish. As usual, his best friend was dressing in a far corner of the room, everyone keeping a distance from the bag of equipment the girls called "The Skunk's Armpit." Nish was burrowing away in it like a raccoon in a garbage bag, pulling out garter straps and old underwear and yellow-stained T-shirts. Travis figured if Nish could stick his head into his own hockey bag without hurling then he must be feeling better. He was back to being Nish, all-star defenceman for the Tamarack Screech Owls.

They were playing in the Macquarie Ice Rink, which was attached to a shopping centre out Waterloo Road. According to Mr. Dillinger, it was the only hockey rink in Sydney. In Canada, a city the size of Sydney would have had dozens. The building was simple but functional, with roomy dressing rooms, the lines and circles in the ice surface freshly painted for the tournament, and air-conditioning powerful enough to keep the ice hard and fast.

They were playing, appropriately, the Sydney

Sharks. They had a logo almost identical to the one worn by the NHL's San Jose Sharks, their socks matched their sweaters, and, from what Travis could make out in the brief warm-up, they had first-rate equipment. Stepping out onto the ice surface, they looked like an elite peewee team from a city like Toronto or Vancouver or Detroit.

It was after they took that first step that the difference was noticeable.

Only three or four of the players could skate as well as the Owls. A couple of them were well over on their ankles. One carried his stick as if it were an alien weapon that had popped through a time warp into his puzzled hands.

Sarah drew even with Travis then spun around to face him as she skated backwards up-ice.

"Check out number 17," she said, before speeding effortlessly away.

Travis followed the direction of Sarah's pointed stick. The Sharks were circling about their own net, firing pucks at random while they waited for their goaltender to take up his position.

Travis would have known who Sarah meant even if he hadn't seen the number flash as the Shark's tallest player curled back towards the net, slapping his stick on the ice for a puck.

Number 17 was tall, with blond curly hair sticking out under the back of his helmet and his jersey tucked into his hockey pants on the right side, Wayne Gretzky style. He moved with a grace that set him apart at once from every one of his teammates. He skated with that strange, bowlegged stride that has been the trademark of so many of hockey's loveliest skaters – Bobby Orr and Gilbert Perreault from the old days, or more recently Alexander Mogilny and Pavel Bure – and he had the same quirky little shoulder shuffle that Sarah sometimes did when she was about to change pace. He was one of those players who seemed naturally at ease with everything he touched: equipment, sweater, stick, skates, ice. A little shuffle, and he shot ahead like he'd come out of a cannon – yet Travis had barely noticed the change in stride.

Number 17 shot, high and hard, ringing the puck off the crossbar and over the glass into the protective netting behind the boards. He raised his glove in a fist.

Travis liked him instantly. He didn't even know number 17's name, but if he had a thing about trying to put pucks off crossbars, Travis knew they already had much in common.

He looked across ice to where Sarah was working on her crossovers along the blueline. There was something different about her. She always did a dance of crossovers across the blueline, but always, always, she faced her own net while doing them. This time she was turned around, closely watching number 17.

Muck blew his whistle hard at centre ice. The

Owls stopped immediately, shovelling the loose pucks back towards the net and heading for their coach, who was standing with the coach of the Sydney Sharks.

The players all arrived at once, most of the Owls using cute little referee stops – one skate turned sideways and tucked behind the other, body tilting back to dig in for a soft stop – while some of the Sharks were using the "snowplough" stop that Travis had last used in initiation hockey.

This wasn't going to be much of a game.

"A little mix-and-match," Muck said, using his whistle to point. "Lindsay, Cuthbertson, Noorizadeh, Staples, Nishikawa – move over and line up on this blueline."

Travis looked at Sarah, who shrugged and pushed over on one leg. Fahd and Jenny and Nish followed.

The other coach called out five names, including the Sharks goaltender, and told them to join the five Owls on the blueline.

Muck looked over, a half grin playing at the corners of his mouth.

"Okay," he said. "Change sweaters, all of you."

The five Sharks were already struggling out of their sweaters. Sarah looked once at Travis, made a quick face, and dropped her gloves to remove her helmet. Travis followed suit, kissing the inside of his sweater as he dragged it back off. None of the Sharks players wore a "C," or even an "A" for assistant captain. He hated giving up his treasured "C" for any reason.

One of the Sharks tossed his sweater at Travis. "Here ya gow, myte," he said, smiling. At first Travis thought the kid was joking, putting on a fake Australian accent, but then he realized it was his actual way of talking – it was just that it sounded much more strange in a hockey rink than it did out in the streets of Sydney.

When the sweaters had been exchanged, the two coaches spoke to their new players.

"Evens things up," the Sydney coach said to the Screech Owls now wearing Sharks jerseys. "Muck tells me you two" – he pointed to Travis and Sarah – "should play with Wiz."

Wiz? Travis wondered. Who the heck was *Wiz?*

"*Wiz?*" Sarah asked, blinking in confusion.

"Him," the coach explained, pointing with his stick towards number 17, who was leaning on his stick, helmet up, smiling back at them.

"That's a funny name," said Sarah.

"His real name's Bruce," laughed the coach. "But the kids all call him Wiz. Short for Wizard, eh?"

"*Wizard?*" Sarah asked, still puzzled.

"Wizard of *Oz*," the coach said. "*Get it?*"

5

IT DIDN'T TAKE THEM LONG TO "GET IT." WITH Muck refereeing while Mr. Dillinger worked the Screech Owls bench, the shinny game got under way with number 17 at centre between Sarah and Travis, and with Fahd and Nish going over to give the Sharks' defence a little depth and Jenny in net to give them a fighting chance.

It felt strange for Travis not to have Sarah at centre and Dmitri flying down right wing, but strange only for the first couple of shifts. By midway through the first period, it felt like he and Sarah had spent their entire lives as wingers for the Wizard of Oz.

Travis had seen talent like this rarely. Certainly Sasha, Dmitri's Russian cousin, had similar skating skills, but this Aussie kid, Wiz, seemed to see the game as well as Sarah herself.

It was almost impossible to get to know anyone in the midst of a hockey game. The three sat together on the bench when their line was off, but they talked little except about plays they might try. Wiz – Travis still had trouble thinking anyone might be called that – was certainly friendly enough, but he was also all business during the game, even if it was a meaningless exhibition match.

"What's the big D's name, mate?" he asked Travis at one point.

"Wayne Nishikawa," Travis said. "Everybody calls him Nish."

"He's bloody good, eh?"

Travis nodded, a bit reluctantly. Nish was in full show-off mode, just as Travis knew he would be in an exhibition match. He was lugging the puck, keeping the puck, trying to score the fancy goals. But Jeremy was hot in the Owls' net, and no matter how much Nish pressed he wasn't able to beat him.

It was a strange game. The players' ability varied widely, but the coaches were careful to keep the weaker lines against each other – Sydney players in Owls sweaters against Sydney players on the Sharks' side – and Travis and Sarah and their new centre against the top Owls lines. Ten minutes into the game, no one had scored a single goal.

Travis couldn't believe some of the things Wiz could do. He had exceptional speed, but he wasn't a glory hog. He'd no sooner get the puck than he'd be looking for either Travis or Sarah on a break, and he used the points brilliantly, cycling pucks in the corner until he saw an opening to fire a pass out to Nish or Fahd or one of the Sydney defenders for a good shot. Wiz and Nish were clearly feeding off each other, trying to outdo each other with the perfect, unexpected pass.

Wiz also had a trick that Travis would have given anything to learn. Just like an NHLer, Wiz could scoop up a puck from the ice, bounce it a couple of times on his stick, catch it dead on the blade, and then hand it over to Muck for a faceoff. Even Muck seemed impressed.

Travis couldn't count the hours that he and Sarah had spent trying to scoop pucks the same way.

Andy Higgins scored first for the Owls on a hard slapper that beat Jenny to the five-hole. Then Simon Milliken scored. Fahd scored on a tip-in, and one of the better Sharks scored on a lucky rebound.

"Well, mates," Wiz said as they sat on the bench waiting for their next shift. "What say we put on a little show for them?"

"You're on," said Sarah, heading over the boards.

They changed on the fly, Sarah racing back to pick up a loose puck that Nish kicked up as a Shark pressed him against the boards behind his net. Sarah turned, reversed directions, and flew around the net and headed up Travis's side.

Travis instinctively crossed over.

Sarah sent a high pass to Wiz, which he knocked down easily with his glove and kicked up onto his stick. He flew up across centre, looking for Travis on the far side.

Travis rapped the ice for a pass, and Wilson, trying to read the play, dove to block the pass everyone thought was coming.

But Wiz faked the pass, dropped the puck back into his skates, and, kicking it back and forth between his blades like a kid with a soccer ball, danced around Sam and moved in alone.

He came in hard, and stopped dead, throwing Jeremy off completely. Without even a glance, he passed back to Sarah, now driving hard for the net. Sarah stickhandled quickly around Jeremy and threw it back to Wiz for the shot.

But Wiz didn't even try to take the puck with his stick. He angled his skates so the puck hit his left blade, then his right, and rebounded perfectly across the crease onto Travis's stick.

The net was completely empty. Travis could have done a math problem he had so much time. He just tucked the puck in and turned to look at Wiz, who was grinning from ear to ear.

"Was that on purpose?" Travis asked as Wiz and the others came to slap his back.

"You'll never know, mate," Wiz answered, laughing.

They had an hour to play. The Owls went ahead, the Sharks caught up. Sarah scored a lovely goal on her usual shoulder-fake move. Dmitri scored a typical Dmitri backhander that shot the water bottle off the net.

"What's the score?" Sarah shouted as they realized time was winding down. The Zamboni driver was already starting up his machine.

"Who knows?" said Wiz.

"I think we need one to win," Travis said.

"One it is, then, mate," Wiz said as the coach called their line for the final faceoff.

Wiz won it easily. He shovelled the puck to Nish, who swung back and around his net, hitting Sarah on the far side.

Sarah passed cross-ice to Travis, who chopped the puck into the middle for Wiz, who was already at full speed.

Wiz hit the blueline in front of Sam and did a perfect "spinnerama" move, leaving Sam on her knees while he spun like a top around her, the puck moving perfectly with him.

Wiz moved in behind the goal, holding the puck. Both Travis and Sarah raced for the sides of the net, trusting in a pass.

Wiz passed to Sarah, who rapped it back.

Wilson tried to take out Wiz, but Wiz bounced the puck off the back of the net as Wilson flew by into the boards.

Sam took out Travis. Andy, coming back hard, took out Sarah. Simon Milliken tied up Nish on the point so he couldn't break for the net and a pass.

Wiz stickhandled so loosely he might have been the only person on the ice. He looked up, smiling.

Travis tried to scramble back, but Sam had too good an angle on him and was too strong for him to break away.

Wiz did his little scoop move, and instantly the puck was lying on his stick blade as if he were about to hand it to the referee.

Is he quitting? Travis wondered. *Did the horn blow?*

But he wasn't quitting. With the puck still balanced perfectly on his blade, Wiz skated out from behind the net, looped the stick in a fake that sent Jeremy over flat on his back, and then *tossed* rather than shot the puck high in under the crossbar.

Muck's whistle and the horn blew at exactly the same time.

The Sharks – and the Owls who were temporary Sharks – mobbed Wiz, who was laughing at what he'd done.

"No fair!" Jeremy was shouting to Muck and slamming his stick on the ice at the same time. "That's illegal."

Muck just shook his head, grinning.

"Never seen a goal like it," he said. "But there's nothing in the rule books to say you can't do it."

6

MURDER, HOWEVER, FOLLOWED NO RULES.
There was nothing fair about it. Nothing to say
who might do it, or how.

Travis wasn't even certain it was murder, though
a head cut clean off certainly suggested foul play.

The facts were obvious: Great White Shark
burps up human head. Obviously, someone had
to die to produce the human head. But no one
knew who, or how, or, for that matter, where all
the other body parts were.

"GRISLY DISCOVERY FOR CANADIAN HOCKEY
VISITORS," said the headline on the front page of
that day's *Sydney Morning Herald*. Below the
headline was a photograph of the Screech Owls
being brought out of the Aquarium by first-aid
workers. Sam was bawling into Sarah's shoulder.
Nish looked like he'd already thrown up.

It was the first time Nish hadn't raced to see
his picture in a newspaper. "Food poisoning," he
kept saying. "But no one will believe me." And
no one did.

By the next day, they had a little more to go on. Police pathologists had determined the head belonged to a male Asian, probably aged between twenty-five and fifty. There had apparently been some minor dental work done on the man's teeth, but the chances of finding the dental records of a man who could have come from anywhere in the world, who was but one of approximately a *billion* men in that age group who could be roughly described as "Asian," were remote if not impossible.

"Who *was* he?" Data kept asking. He had used his laptop to connect to the Internet and had scoured every Southeast Asian newspaper he could find published in English to see if a man had gone missing at sea, but he'd come up with nothing.

The police weren't much further ahead. Mr. Dillinger had phoned them to ask if they had any new information. The poor shark had been drugged so it could be examined, but an X-ray and ultrasound had indicated no other human body parts inside, which meant the shark had somehow scooped up the head as it fell down through the water or else while it lay on the sea bottom. According to the Sydney coroner, marks on the neck area suggested the head had been severed by something other than shark's teeth.

"Which means," Data added, "that the man was decapitated."

Mr. Dillinger grimaced. He didn't like to put it that way, but obviously, the man's head had come off somehow. In a terrible boating accident? Struck by a propeller? Caught on an anchor line?

"Chopped off with a machete!" Fahd offered.

Mr. Dillinger just looked at Fahd, the team manager's big, wrinkled face looking sad and anxious for a change of topic.

"But why?" Sam asked.

"And *who*?" Sarah added.

That morning, the Owls set out for Homebush Bay, the site of the Summer Olympic Games. They took the Green line train out to Lidcombe Station, then switched to the Yellow line that looped out around Olympic Park and back.

It was another beautiful day. Travis was already beginning to notice a major difference about Australians. No one here ever talked about the weather. At home it was almost a constant topic of conversation – *Will it last? Enjoy it while it's here! What's the forecast?* But in Sydney the weather seemed entirely taken for granted. If every day was bright and warm, if every sky was blue, what was the point in discussing it?

Olympic Park was fantastic. They walked along the waterways and parks around the site and saw where the Olympic Athletes Village had been. They toured the Olympic pool with its high, jagged "shark's fin" architecture. They saw the Olympic Stadium where the stunning opening ceremonies had been held and the Olympic Flame lit.

There were other peewee teams already there, all of them excitedly preparing for the Mini-Olympics part of the tournament, and if Travis thought some of the Australian players looked out of their element on ice, they certainly looked at home here.

"I think I'll try pole vault," Dmitri said.

Several of the Owls went over to the pole vault area with Dmitri to watch. He picked out a thin, flexible pole, paced off his run, walked back once to measure the height he'd need to clear the bar, walked out, paused, and then ran, dropping the tip of the pole so it caught and whipped him high, perfectly shooting his legs up and away before releasing the pole while he floated easily over the bar.

"Is there anything Dmitri can't do?" Sam asked, laughing and cheering with the rest.

They spent much of the afternoon trying out different venues and equipment. Dmitri and Sarah kept pretty much to the track. Fahd went over to the archery field with Lars. Jeremy and Gordie Griffith spent time in the basketball court pretending they were Vince Carter and trying to slam-dunk off a small trampoline that some of the workers had set up in front of one of the nets. Derek and Jesse took on Liz and Jenny in doubles tennis at the same courts where Serena and Venus Williams had won the gold medal in doubles.

Everybody was busy but one lonely Screech Owl: Wayne Nishikawa. He wouldn't join Travis at the handball courts. He wouldn't play tennis. He wouldn't go with Fahd to the archery. Sarah asked him if he wanted to swim in the Olympic pool, but he wasn't interested. Sam asked him if the two of them should work on their diving, but he said he wasn't ready.

"Look," Travis said, "if you had your choice of anything, what would you do?"

Nish didn't miss a beat. "Go to Bondi Beach."

Travis remembered that Bondi Beach, on the other side of the city, was where they had held the beach volleyball competition. But hadn't they torn down the volleyball stadium when it was over?

"There's nothing there," Travis said.

"That's what *you* think," Nish said.

Travis watched in astonishment as Nish dug deep into his wallet and produced a page torn from a Sydney guide book he must have picked up in the hotel lobby. He carefully unfolded the page and handed it over, a look of triumph on his beaming face.

Travis took the page, and saw at once what had caught his friend's eye.

No visit to Sydney is complete without a visit to Australia's most famous beach. But visitors be warned – Nude Sunbathing is Everywhere at Bondi!

Travis handed the crumpled page back to Nish.

"You never give up, do you?"

"Everyone has a calling in life," smiled Nish. "Some become priests. Some become doctors or teachers. I'm a natural-born nudist."

"C'mon," Travis suggested, changing the topic, "the girls are at the diving pool. Let's at least check it out."

They headed along the wide Olympic Boulevard until they came to the International Aquatic Centre. A side door was open for the visiting peewee teams, and they raced up the steps and in. The building took Travis's breath away when he saw how massive it was inside. It seemed there were as many seats as in an NHL hockey rink. The Olympic pool was at one end, with the medal podium still there beside it. At the far end of the building was the diving pool, with the one-metre and three-metre boards flanking the high tower. From where Travis stood, the tower appeared as high as a bungee jump – only with nothing but the water below to break your fall.

"*Come on up!*" a voice called.

Travis and Nish scanned high into the ceiling. It was Sarah at the very top of the tower. She was wearing a red maple leaf Canadian swimsuit, and her hair was dripping wet. *Had she already jumped?*

"KKKAAAA–WWWAAAA–BUNGAAAA!"

The jungle cry came from behind Sarah. A blur of red roared past her – red swimsuit, red hair, red face – and out onto the diving platform. It spun once in a perfect somersault and plummeted down, down, down, to crash into the water with a splash so big it reached Travis and Nish.

Sam.

"That must have stung," said Nish.

But before Travis could answer, the water broke again, wet red hair flying, fist pumping, red face defiant.

"EEEEEEE–AAWWWWWW–KEEEEEEE!"

"She's insane," Nish said matter-of-factly. Sam, yelling the same stupid yells Nish always yelled. Sam, the centre of attention just like Nish always had to be. But according to Nish, *she* was the insane one.

Sam swam to where the two boys stood and eased out of the pool. She walked right by them and headed straight back to the tower, hands on her hips, water dripping in a trail behind her.

"You here for our practice, Big Boy?" she called over her shoulder to Nish.

"Didn't bring a bathing suit," Nish answered, flustered.

"Since when did *that* ever stop you?" Sarah yelled down from high up the tower.

Then she jumped, as graceful in mid-air as she was on the ice, as completely in control falling as she ever was skating or running. She completed a perfect jackknife, then opened up to slice into the water with hardly a ripple.

"She's good," said Sam, nodding in approval.

"She's good at everything," said Travis.

"I gotta get going," Nish said. He was already walking towards the door.

"What about our practice?" Sam yelled.

"Later," Nish said. "It'll have to be later. I'm busy right now."

Travis stared after his friend. He had seen a familiar look in Nish's eyes. It had nothing to do with being "busy." Nish was just terrified of heights – almost as much as he was afraid of being laughed at.

7

THERE WAS A NOTE WAITING AT THE FRONT DESK for Sarah and Travis when they came down for breakfast the next morning:

Dear linemates!

My dad is taking the boat out today. We've room and snorkelling equipment for the three of us and four more. Check with your coach – my dad has already called.

Wiz

"*Seahorses!*" Sarah shouted. "*Finally, I'm going to get to see real wild seahorses!*"

She ran straight back to her room to tell the other girls. Travis figured he should check first with Muck. The Screech Owls coach said he had indeed got a call, and there was no problem with it as far as he was concerned. Wiz's father, it turned out, was a former NHL player, Des Roberts, who'd ended up working in Australia helping build ice surfaces, and now lived here permanently. Muck and he had even known each other back in junior days.

"He's fully certified for diving," said Muck. "So's his wife, and she's going along, too. So off with you – and enjoy yourselves."

Wiz had said there would be room for Sarah and Travis and four more. Sarah was bringing Sam and Jenny. Travis figured he'd ask Fahd and Nish.

"*Snorkelling?*" Nish said, rolling the word around his tongue like it was something a pig wouldn't swallow.

"Yeah," Travis said. "C'mon. You took that course – here's your chance."

Nish shrugged. The previous winter Travis had talked him into signing up for scuba lessons at the local pool. Sarah had taken the lessons too, and though all had learned how to use air tanks well enough to pass the course, none of them had dived anywhere but in the pool.

"I'm up for it!" shouted Fahd.

"We have to go out in a boat?" Nish asked.

"Get real," Travis said, losing his patience. "You want us to swim out the harbour?"

But Travis knew what Nish was getting at. He really did have a weak stomach. He didn't like heights. He didn't like being at sea.

But Travis knew how to get him. "Sam's going," he said. "You wouldn't want her to think you're chicken, would you?"

Nish reddened a bit, then suddenly brightened.

"What about snorkelling at Bondi Beach?" he suggested.

A horrific picture formed immediately in Travis's mind. Women out for a topless swim suddenly screaming and racing for shore, everyone convinced it must be a shark – until the big, sunburnt back of a snorkelling Nish rises from the waters, grin wider than his face mask.

"We're going farther than that," said Travis. "Grab your suit and let's get going."

Nish didn't move. He seemed undecided.

Finally, he headed over to his pile of clothes on the floor, kicked several times at the heap, reached in deep, and came up with his beloved Mighty Ducks of Anaheim swimsuit. It was a piece of clothing, Travis noticed, that Nish far preferred to throw off than pull on.

They took off from the marina at Mosman Bay, almost directly across the big harbour from the Opera House. Mr. Roberts had a beautiful boat. It was pure white, with sleeping quarters below for eight, a small galley for cooking, and even a tiny washroom. The boat was outfitted for deep-sea fishing and cruising, with an elevated bridge for the controls and a high antenna for radio communication and navigation. It was called *Puck*, a name that Travis figured would have been lost on every person who had ever seen the boat – right up until the moment the Screech Owls came aboard.

Wiz and his parents were great hosts. They had hamburgers and hot dogs cooking on the barbecue on deck, and a cooler full of ice-cold Cokes ready to go the moment they left the marina. The kids ate and drank as the Robertses took turns showing off the various sights. They passed by the Taronga Zoo – Nish claimed he could see giraffes staring out above the trees – and saw where the prime minister and the governor-general lived. Then, with the towering Sydney Harbour Bridge growing smaller in their wake, they headed out through the mouth of the harbour into the open sea, where they turned right – *starboard*, Travis reminded himself – to travel due south along the high rocks of the oceanside bluffs.

The ocean was rolling. The big boat rode the swells nicely and moved at a good pace. Travis checked Nish, who seemed in fine spirits. He was standing at the bow, the wind blowing his black hair straight back, and he was smiling as he watched the shoreline.

Finally he pointed. "*Bondi Beach?*" he called up to Mr. Roberts, who was standing on the bridge with Wiz, the two of them consulting a chart.

Mr. Roberts – a big man with large hands and a crooked nose he said proved he'd once played in the NHL – looked up, stared hard towards shore, and then nodded back at Nish.

"*You got binoculars?*" Nish shouted.

Wiz hurried down from the bridge with the binoculars, holding them out for Nish.

"How powerful are they?" Nish asked. He seemed almost frantic.

"Real good, mate," said Wiz. "What d'ya want 'em for?"

"*Topless sunbathers!*" Sam shouted from the other side of the boat.

"*You have a mental case on your boat, you know!*" added Sarah.

"You're sure he's not an Aussie?" Wiz laughed. "He sure acts like an Aussie bloke!"

Nish almost yanked the binoculars away from Wiz. He put them to his eyes, adjusted the focus, and leaned out in a desperate effort to get closer to the fabled beach.

Wiz held on to Nish's shoulder to make sure he didn't end up as shark bait.

Nish scanned the shoreline back and forth.

"*See anything?*" Sam called.

"They're not *strong* enough!" Nish whined.

"Sorry about that, mate," laughed Wiz. "You'll just have to make do with some topless seahorses, I guess."

"*And they're the men!*" Sarah and Jenny shrieked together.

"Very funny," Nish grumbled.

"Very, very funny."

8

THEY CRUISED FOR NEARLY TWO HOURS, THE sun warming their backs and dancing off the crests of the gentle swells. It was a beautiful day, the sky sprinkled with curious gulls riding the wind currents high above the boat and the air so warm the kids were soon stripped down to just their swimsuits and a thick layer of sunscreen.

Mr. and Mrs. Roberts were the kind of parents a kid only dreams of: rock music blared from speakers set up on either side of the bridge, the cooler was never out of cold pop, and they had enough chocolate bars and licorice to satisfy even the world's number-one sweet tooth, which belonged, of course, to Nish.

Nish was holding up well. He had his Oakley sunglasses sitting perfectly on the peak of his brand-new Billabong baseball cap. He had his Mighty Ducks swimsuit on, and he lay, stomach down, on a huge beach towel, his legs waving in the air while he pounded out the beat on the deck with one fist and held a giant half-eaten Oh Henry! chocolate bar in the other.

Nothing green about Nish's gills, Travis thought. At least not yet.

Nish, however, was not the centre of attention. That honour went to Wiz, who was entertaining the girls with a little air concert, hopping around the deck on one foot while he picked out a wild imaginary guitar solo. Sam and Sarah and Jenny were all up and dancing to the music. Fahd had a couple of wooden salad spoons out and was playing along on the drums. Mrs. Roberts must have noticed the salad spoons, but she was saying nothing. Wiz and his new friends were welcome to enjoy themselves any way they wished.

"*Up ahead!*" Mr. Roberts shouted from the bridge.

Travis got up from the towel where he was lying beside Nish and put his hand above his eyes, trying to shield them from the sun. It was almost impossible to see, the way the sun was skipping off the waves, but eventually the boat swung to the port side and Travis was able to make out what lay ahead.

It was an island out of a movie. It lay like a pearl-encircled emerald in the sparkling blue ocean. The sand looked almost white. On each side rocks rose from the sand up to a plateau, where trees seemed to wave at them in the light wind coming out of the east.

Mr. Roberts let up on the throttle and eased farther to port, as though he planned to circle the island. Travis couldn't understand why. If ever he had seen a natural landing site, it was dead ahead, on the sand.

"*There's the reef!*" Mrs. Roberts yelled out. She was leaning over the bow, straining to see, golden curls – exactly the same as Wiz's – bouncing in the wind.

Mr. Roberts nodded and swung the wheel hard, bringing the boat around in a full circle.

"*Drop anchor!*" he shouted.

Wiz immediately set to work. He called Fahd and Travis over to help him throw the anchor over the side, then pushed a button that released the anchor cable. The anchor struck the bottom, and he pushed the button again, setting it securely.

The boat slowed and stopped, rocking in the gentle waves.

"We're going to dive here!" Mr. Roberts called down to the kids. "After, we'll take the inflatable in to the beach for a little picnic. Okay?"

"*O-kay!*" the Owls shouted together.

Wiz was already hauling out the gear. There were masks, fins, snorkels, gloves, even a couple of large underwater flashlights.

"You've all snorkelled before?" Mr. Roberts asked.

"Sure."

"Yeah."

"Travis and Nish and I have our scuba diving certificates," Sarah said.

"You do?" Mrs. Roberts said, surprised.

"But we've only ever done it in a pool," added Travis.

"Well," Mr. Roberts said, pleased. "Wiz and I dive, too. And I think we've got enough equipment to go around – maybe the five of us will get out if we've time."

First, though, they snorkelled. The three girls went with Mr. Roberts, the three boys with Wiz, all of them advised not to touch a thing unless either Mr. Roberts or Wiz said it was all right. Mrs. Roberts would stay in the boat so she could help out in an emergency.

"I've a good book," she told them. "I'm perfectly happy right here."

Travis put his equipment on, sat on the ledge just above the water at the stern, and let himself fall in backwards, the same way he'd been taught to enter the water while scuba diving.

But he'd never felt water like this before. It seemed, somehow, brighter and lighter than any water he had swum in before. He'd snorkelled all over his grandparents' little lake at the cottage, but that water was dark even if you looked at it in a glass, and it was impossible to see down more than ten or twelve feet. This was more like a pool – but better. He could taste the saltwater on his lips. He could feel it stinging where he'd scraped his shin on the coffee table in the hotel room. But it also felt so clean, almost as if he were being scrubbed by the ocean as he moved through it with his head down, his arms dangling by his side, and his legs lightly kicking.

It seemed he could see forever. The light slipped and shook down through the water and bounced off the bottom. He could see plants moving, and fish – more fish than he had ever imagined possible – moving in and out of coral banks that were themselves so vibrant he could barely believe the colours.

There were pink and orange sponges, all of them moving so slowly in the water it seemed they were swaying to music. There were brilliant fire-red beds of soft coral, and dark, brainlike stands of hard coral. Wiz used a thumbs-up or thumbs-down signal to let them know what could be lightly touched and what should be avoided. It seemed to Travis that half the creatures they were seeing had stingers. He wondered how Wiz ever kept them all straight. He hoped he could.

With Wiz leading the way, they moved into shallower waters and began diving down to pick up shells and crabs and examine them. At one point Wiz grabbed a green turtle by the back legs and swam with it, aiming towards Nish, who turned suddenly, screamed a huge wall of bubbles, and headed fast for the surface. A moment later, he was back down again, as enchanted by the colours and light and sea creatures as the rest of them.

The two groups swam together for a while. Wiz dove down deep and came back up with a large orange sea star, which he handed to Sarah. She took it as if it were a flower and gently carried it back to the bottom and set it down.

A shadow moved off to the right!

Travis turned, startled. A huge ray was swimming beside him, the fin closest to Travis lifting like a huge, lazy wing as it turned away.

Mr. Roberts expertly grabbed onto the ray as it passed, a hand on each of the huge fish's "shoulders," and rode it along for a while.

He signalled Nish to come and join him.

Nish scrambled deeper, his motions rough and awkward compared to the extraordinary elegance of the big fish.

Mr. Roberts held the ray tight while Nish placed his hands where Mr. Roberts' had been. Once Nish had a grip, Mr. Roberts let go.

The big fish moved off, hauling Nish, kicking madly, with it. It saw Sarah and Sam, drifting just in front while they watched and laughed at Nish, and it turned abruptly, almost throwing him off.

But Nish held tight. The ray came straight at Travis, saw him, and banked again. Travis stared into his friend's face. He saw fear and total joy at the same time.

Nish opened his mouth wide, bubbles scattering.

Travis heard a muffled roar, Nish shouting.

"KAAAAAA-(*gulp*)-WWWAAAAAA-(*gulp*)-BUNGAAAAA!"

9

"YOU REALLY WANT TO SEE SEAHORSES, DO YOU?"
Mr. Roberts asked after they'd all come back to
the boat for a rest.

"More than anything else," said Sarah.

"There's some thick seagrass growing just off
the far side of the island. I've seen them in there.
I've also seen the odd seadragon there."

"*Seadragon?*" said Sarah, her brow furrowing.

"You like seahorses," said Mr. Roberts, "you'll
love seadragons. They're very rare, and found
only in these waters. Only place in the world, as
a matter of fact. They're like seahorses – both are
what they call pipefish – only a million times
more exotic. There's two types – the Weedy
Seadragon and the Leafy Seadragon, which is
even weirder-looking. Think of something
that's half seahorse and half Christmas tree and
you'll be close. Once you see one, you'll never
forget it."

"*And they're here!*" Sarah said.

"I've seen some. Can't guarantee it, but if you
and the other kids want to try fitting on that

scuba equipment in the hold, I'll take you down for a look."

"*YESSSS!*" Sarah shouted, then immediately blushed with embarrassment.

Travis wasn't certain it was such a good idea. Sure, they knew how to scuba dive, but their only experience had been in the town pool, where the greatest danger lay in slipping on the soap in the shower. Here, there were moray eels and poisonous jellyfish and stingrays and killer puffers and, of course, the most dangerous shark in the oceans, the Great White.

But Mr. Roberts and Wiz said they knew the reef and the island and the seaweed beds beyond as well as they knew their own backyard.

"*Better!*" said Wiz. "The only time I'm ever in the backyard is when I'm mowing the lawn!"

Mrs. Roberts and the others set off in the inflatable boat across the coral reef to the beach. Mr. Roberts, Wiz, Sarah, Nish, and Travis pulled up the anchor and took a wide, safe sweep around the island before anchoring again.

The light was different here. Instead of bouncing and rippling off the bottom, it seemed to die in a dark green ebbing and flowing mass that was the seagrass.

They suited up, checked their air, and dropped again into the water. They went down deep and stayed deep. The only sound Travis could hear was coming from his own bubbles.

Travis found the training coming back to him. The tank at first felt cumbersome on his back, but soon he grew used to it and he could slip along the bottom almost like the ray Nish had been riding. A small shift of his shoulders and he could turn; a single flick of one flipper and he could shift directions. In and out of the seaweed clumps he twisted and turned, feeling more a part of the ocean than he had imagined possible.

There were small fish everywhere, bright silvery ones that moved in huge schools, rainbow-coloured ones that slipped in and out of coral caves. Sarah and Wiz came across a school – a *herd*? – of seahorses and waved the others over, and they watched the funny little creatures almost bouncing along the currents as they moved through the seagrass.

To his far left Travis saw Mr. Roberts signalling. He had his finger up to his mouthpiece. He wanted them to move carefully.

Down into the waving grass they followed him, until he came to a stop before a large clump growing above a huge chunk of white coral.

He parted several strands and pointed.

Inside, moving along a floating blade of grass, was the strangest creature Travis had ever seen.

It looked a bit like a seahorse that had been through a wringer. Its head was miniature, its "ears" seemed like something from a space movie. It looked as if it were dressed all over in little leaves, the greenish gold fronds fluttering like hummingbird wings as the slender creature moved.

Mr. Roberts held out a finger and the seadragon cozied up to it, wrapping its odd leafy tail about his finger. He moved the exquisite little creature over directly in front of Sarah's mask.

Travis could see Sarah's eyes. They were wide and as alive as the creature itself. She was in love!

Wiz pointed off in the distance. There were more seadragons moving through the grasses. He pointed again. More still!

They split up. Wiz, Nish, and Travis followed a small group of seadragons as they moved, half swimming, half drifting, along a steep slope down into deeper waters, where more weed rippled in the distance. It seemed there were seadragons everywhere. They floated around the boys like falling snowflakes.

Wiz pointed to a huge green turtle that had been roused by the human invaders and was quickly moving away along the sandy bottom.

The boys gave chase, just able to keep pace with their flippers. He was huge, big enough for them all to hitch a ride on, and they began chasing harder.

The turtle turned sharply, vanishing under a mass of weed and through a narrow gap in the rocks.

Wiz made the turn perfectly.

Nish missed, and took the long way around.

Travis followed Wiz, reaching out to grab the rocks and propel himself through the opening.

Wiz had caught the turtle by one large fin. He was indicating that Travis should take the other.

Travis moved swiftly. He seized the large flipper and was instantly surprised by the strength of the animal. But he held fast.

The turtle kept swimming, oblivious to his two hitchhikers. They were moving quickly. Travis turned, and Wiz gave a thumbs-up with his free hand. Travis didn't have the confidence to loosen his grip, so he smiled a burst of bubbles. Wiz laughed, his face vanishing in his own bubbles.

It was like flying. Over banks of coral and down tight to the sand they sped. Through long funnels of grass and in between the rocks.

Finally Wiz let go, and Travis did the same. The turtle, without so much as a look back, vanished into the deeper, darker waters.

The two boys turned towards each other, laughing and high-fiving until they realized they were alone.

No Nish.

10

TRAVIS'S FIRST INSTINCT WAS TO PANIC. HE AND Wiz had been so caught up in their ride they had ignored the first rule of diving: *stick together.* Travis was in unknown territory, but at least he was with Wiz.

Nish, on the other hand, was completely out of his element.

Wiz must have seen the fear in Travis's eyes. He took Travis's shoulders in his hands and squeezed tight. He indicated that Travis should follow him, and set off in the direction they had come, kicking hard.

They swam for what seemed a long time. Travis knew they had begun with at least twenty minutes of air time, probably more, but he had no idea how much they had used up. *Maybe Nish was already out of air!* He realized he was panicking, and that panic simply used up valuable air, so he forced himself to slow his breathing and concentrate on following Wiz.

Travis thought he recognized some of the rock structures and began to calm down. Nish was probably already back at the boat. He was probably already into his second cold Coke, laughing at Travis for wasting so much good pop and chocolate time by swimming around after a stupid turtle.

They breached the same tight rock formation where they had lost Nish, but no one was there.

They moved through the floating seagrass, past a scurrying school of seadragons, and on over the ledge into shallower water.

Just before the rise, Travis thought he saw something out of the corner of his eye. Then he realized that Wiz was turning abruptly in the same direction, bubbles boiling up around his head.

It was Nish!

But not alone. Another diver had Nish in a headlock and was violently twisting Nish's neck. He was trying to knock Nish's air hose out of his mouth.

Travis was confused. Another diver? Where had he come from?

Wiz was already onto the attacker. He was larger than Wiz, but not by much, and Wiz was moving so quickly he seemed to catch the diver off guard. The man must have loosened his grip, because Nish was able to break away.

Travis knew he had to tend first to his friend, who looked in total terror. His hose had popped free and he was making no effort to put it back.

Travis grabbed Nish's flailing arms and held them tight. He looked sternly into his eyes and tried to send him a message: *Settle down, do as I tell you*.

He held onto Nish with one hand and used the other to grab the air hose, which was floating freely now. He shoved it back into Nish's mouth. Nish choked, but then began gulping. He was getting air.

Travis could feel the panic letting go of his friend's body. Nish sagged immediately, and Travis realized how exhausted he must be. He must get him to the surface.

Travis began pushing his friend up. He checked down and saw that Wiz was holding his own with the attacker. They were struggling hand-to-hand, both twisting violently, but Wiz was not being thrown around.

If he can just hold on, Travis thought, *I'll come right back to help*.

He kicked as hard as he could. Nish burst through the surface first, spitting out his mouthpiece and screaming at the same time.

"*HHHEEELLLLLPPPPPPPP!!!*"

The boat wasn't too far away. Travis saw Mr. Roberts spinning the wheel and turning in their direction. The anchor was already up. He and Sarah had probably been looking for them, worrying.

Travis left Nish and dived back down, kicking hard, his heart pounding alarmingly as he headed back.

The man was trying the same move on Wiz. He had him in a headlock and was pulling hard at Wiz's air hose, but Wiz was refusing to give in.

Travis kicked hard and drove his head as hard as he could straight into the man's gut.

The attacker doubled over, letting go of Wiz.

There was more movement in the water. Bubbles and swirling arms and legs. For a moment, Travis couldn't make out what it was.

Then he saw Mr. Roberts, wearing only his bathing suit and in his bare feet, kicking as hard as he could at the attacker.

The man pushed once at Wiz, turned, and fled, his flippers allowing him to outdistance Mr. Roberts, who was fast running out of breath and already headed for the surface.

Travis reached out and took Wiz's elbow, but Wiz shook him off and headed back down to the ocean floor.

He pulled at something that raised a cloud of sand. It was a net bag, almost covered by the sandstorm the fight had stirred up.

He held it up, shaking it so the sand washed away.

It was filled with seadragons.

Dozens of seadragons.

And most of them were already dead.

11

"I DON'T UNDERSTAND."

Mr. Roberts seemed to speak for them all. Everyone, including those who had gone to the beach to set up for the picnic, had returned to the boat. They were gathered now on the deck, the net bag had been carefully placed into the fishing boat's live well, and the last of the living seadragons had been gently lifted out by Mrs. Roberts and Sarah and returned to their natural habitat.

But most of the tiny, delicate creatures were dead. They must have been stuffed very roughly into the bag, or crushed to death as the man had hauled the bag around behind him as he searched for more of the wonderful little pipefish.

"I just don't understand," Mr. Roberts repeated. "If he was taking them to sell to collectors, why would he not be more careful? He must have known he was killing them."

"It's so cruel," Sarah said, her voice breaking.

"What exactly happened down there?" Mr. Roberts asked Nish. "Why would he attack you?"

Nish seemed near tears himself. There were huge red welts about his neck and shoulders where the man had wrestled with him. His voice was choked when he spoke, and his hands shook.

"I lost sight of Trav and Wiz," Nish said uncertainly. "I tried to catch up to them, but they were after that turtle and I lost them in the seaweed. So I just circled back, heading for the boat. And when I got into the shallow water I came up behind this guy – I thought it was you, Mr. Roberts – and when I started swimming fast towards him, he turned. He must have thought I was attacking him or something."

"Why would he think *anyone* was attacking him?" Travis asked. "He must have been doing something that he shouldn't have been doing."

"Obviously," said Mrs. Roberts. "He was killing these little things for no reason at all."

"How did he get here?" Wiz asked. "You can't swim here from the mainland."

"There was a boat on the other side of the island," Mrs. Roberts said. "We saw it from the beach."

"What kind of boat?" Mr. Roberts asked.

"I'm not sure," Mrs. Roberts said. "I think I might have a picture of it, though. I was using the video camera, and I think I might have panned it."

"I'll look later," Mr. Roberts said. He seemed dejected. What had been planned as a wonderful adventure suddenly had a sour taste to it.

Travis looked down at the tragedy the man had left behind. The little seadragons didn't look like they could ever have been real. Lifeless, they no longer contained the magic that Travis and the others had felt. They seemed like something grade-school kids might have made with pipe cleaners, a little bit of soggy green paper, scissors, and glue.

Why would the man do this? Travis wondered. It made no sense at all.

They cruised back in silence. No rock music and very little talk, except for what was necessary. Travis grew sleepy with the growl of the engine and the steady slap of the waves on the bow of the Robertses' boat. Sarah sat with the seadragons, carefully lifting them one by one, smoothing out each one and holding it in the palm of her hand before she slipped it over the side, giving it its own private burial at sea.

Nish didn't look so good. So far, for him, Australia had been a series of stomach upsets. He had thrown up after seeing the head burped out of the Great White – "food poisoning," he still maintained – and his stomach was once again rolling like the sea. He had moved as far forward as possible, leaning directly out over the bow and trying to look far into the distance, avoiding the steady tilt and drop and tilt again of the ocean.

"You all right?" Wiz asked him.

"Fine," said Nish, with a look that said otherwise.

"I'll get my dad to pull closer to shore," Wiz said. "If you can fix on the shoreline, you'll feel better. It works for me."

Nish nodded, gathered his strength, and spoke again. "Can he get real close?" he said, pausing to let his bucking stomach settle again. "And can I have the binoculars back?"

Wiz stared a moment at the green-gilled visitor. He shook his head in amazement.

"You're not sick at all, are you?" Wiz finally said, smiling.

"You're wrong on that one," Sarah said.

Wiz hadn't seen her come up behind them. She was also checking on Nish.

"*Sick* is the only way to describe him."

12

"FASCINATING."

Data had his wheelchair tight to the desk in his room and was working on his laptop computer. He and Fahd had spent hours on the Internet ever since the kids had returned from their diving trip with their incredible tale of the dead seadragons and Nish's attacker.

Data had checked out Web sites all over the world. He had sent off e-mails and already had a couple of answers. Now he had compiled his own file and was scrolling down the screen, telling the rest of the Screech Owls the essentials of what he and Fahd had found out.

"No wonder people are fascinated by seahorses," Data said.

"The only males in the world who have babies," Fahd added unnecessarily.

"There's one – they even have a name for him, James – who gave birth to 1,572 babies at once."

"Another world record for you to go after, eh, Nish?" said Sam, giggling.

"*Get a life!*" Nish snapped.

"There's a huge world trade in seahorses," Data said. "They dry them out and grind them into powder to feed to people. They're used in traditional Chinese medicine for everything from curing asthma to restoring energy to old people.

"Says here that forty-five *tonnes* of seahorses are consumed each year in Asia – that's sixteen million of them!"

"Impossible!" Sarah gasped.

"It's true," said Data. "There's all kinds of myths about them, mostly to do with the males giving birth, which some people take as proof of male superiority. Some also believe that the sea-horse can heal itself spontaneously. That's proba-bly because they can grow back their tails if an attacker snaps it off, but not instantly."

"Anyway," Fahd added, jumping in, "you can see why so many might be eaten and why they're so valuable. A little bowl of seahorse soup will cost you four hundred and fifty dollars in a restau-rant in Taiwan."

"A bowl of *soup*?" Sam said. "You can't be serious?"

"I am," said Fahd. "In some places, a kilogram of seahorse powder can go for as high as fifteen thousand dollars."

"They must be nearly extinct!" said Jesse.

"No," said Data. "There are thirty-two differ-ent species, and they're found all around the world. Only one is on the endangered species list."

"What about seadragons?" Sarah asked. "That's what he had. Seadragons, not seahorses."

Fahd nodded. "We know that."

Data cleared his throat. "There's almost nothing on the Web about them. Apparently they're found only in Australia. There are two different species in the world and both exist right here. Even in Sydney Harbour. But they're quite rare, apparently, especially the Leafy Seadragon."

"That's what we saw!" Travis interrupted.

"Well, there's not much we can tell you about them. The Threatened Species Network is trying to have them put on the protected list, but so far they've had no luck."

"What about Chinese medicine?" Andy asked.

"Hardly even mentioned," said Data, scrolling down to the bottom. "One article says they're considered to have even more power than the seahorse. *Ten times* the power. Supposed to cure all the same things, but also give a person incredible courage."

"Hardly seemed a courageous thing to me," Sarah sniffed. "Grabbing them and stuffing them into a bag so they die."

"I know," Fahd agreed. "But that must have been what he was up to. Collecting them to sell on the black market."

"But why attack Nish?" Travis asked. "What did he think Nish was — a cop?"

"We'll never know," said Sarah, shaking her head. "I guess we'll just never know."

13

THEY PLAYED AGAINST THE BRISBANE BANDITS
the following day. Fahd, of course, asked where
Brisbane was, and when Muck said it was quite a
ways north of Sydney, Simon jumped in to say if
it was more north, then the chances were they
might be better hockey players. That seemed to
make sense, until Data explained that the farther
north you go in Australia the hotter it gets.
Darwin, in the far north of Australia, was sur-
rounded by rain forest and had tropical weather
all year round.

"That figures," said Nish, noisily wrapping
clear tape around the tops of his skates. "Everything's always backwards here."

Muck couldn't resist. "Is that a request to play
forward, Nishikawa?"

"No way!" said Nish, reddening. "You can't
be serious?"

"Sure I am," Muck said. "Great opportunity
for us all to try new things. Whatdya say? You're
always racing up the ice anyway when you
shouldn't be, so why not *start* out of position to
save yourself a little time?"

Nish groaned, placing his face in his beefy hands.

"Tell me this isn't happening," he mumbled to himself.

But Muck was serious. He had already juggled the lineup and put their new positions down on a card, so it wasn't just a sudden idea. Travis was now on defence, paired with Dmitri. Lars was another centre, playing between Sam and Fahd. Sarah was back with Andy. Everyone else was also changed. Left wingers became right wingers. Right wingers moved left.

"This is madness," grumbled Nish.

"It'll keep you alert," said Muck. "You can fall into a rut playing all the time with the same person or in the same position. Maybe now you'll find out why so many forwards can't seem to make it back to backcheck."

They finished dressing and took to the ice. The Bandits were already out there, spinning around in their own zone. They stared in something close to awe at the Owls coming out onto the ice. Travis could sort of see why. His team looked marvellous in their matching sweaters and socks, their Screech Owls logos, and each sweater with the player's name over the number – Travis with "Lindsay, 7" and that treasured C just a bit above his pounding heart.

None of the Bandits could skate like Sarah. None had Andy's size or Nish's shot. But they were clearly a better team than the Sydney Sharks, most of whom – Wiz included – were in the stands to watch.

Travis had one of those days. He hit the cross-bar on his first shot in the warm-up, and when the game got underway, he had no trouble at all on defence, in part because the Bandits were slow, and in part because Dmitri was so fast he could make it back in time to cover up if either he or Travis got caught cheating.

Muck seemed remarkably relaxed. He knew that the Owls would never meet a team as good as them over here, and he seemed determined to make it fun for everyone. This wasn't a true tour-nament, after all, just a series of exhibition matches. The Owls were under strict orders not to run up the scores, and Muck gave them per-mission to try all the things they'd be afraid to try in real games back home.

For Nish, now a centre, this was a licence to go insane. He took it upon himself to carry the puck whenever he was on the ice, no matter how thick the traffic. He spun and danced and dipsy-doodled with the puck. He tried spinneramas and even, at one point, deliberately fell onto his knee pads and slid right between the Bandits' defence while choking up on his stick and still stickhandling.

The others were less flashy. Travis tried his backpass a couple of times, and Dmitri read it perfectly. He tried his fancy puck-off-the-skates play, and it worked twice. He even tried the heel pass Bad Joe Hall had taught him, and it worked.

Sarah, on defence, put on a skating spectacular. She was up and down the ice so fast it must have seemed to the Bandits that there were two Sarahs out on the ice, one playing up and one back.

Every time Sarah made an interesting play, the Sharks erupted with cheers, led by Wiz. Sarah was obviously their favourite – or maybe, Travis couldn't help but wonder, just *Wiz*'s favourite.

The Bandits took a while to adjust to the Owls' speed, and they certainly lacked their skill, but they were eager and persistent.

With the Owls up 3–0, Nish tried a foolish lob pass to himself that one of the Bandit defenders read, stepping forward and batting the puck out of the air before it could land. It flew into open ice, and the little Brisbane defenceman raced for it, picking up his own hand pass, which was legal, and then heading up-ice against Dmitri and Travis.

Dmitri had the angle to keep the defenceman cut off from the net, and Travis flew across ice to try to check the puck away from him. The little player threw a pass backhand, blind, but it landed perfectly on the tape of a scurrying Bandits forward, who now had a clear run in on Jenny.

Panicking, he shot, and Jenny kicked it out with a pad, right back onto the blade of the shooter. He shot again, and this time it hit Jenny in the side and pushed on through, dropping on the ice and rolling into the net.

Owls 3, Bandits 1.

The Brisbane bench emptied. They rushed the scorer and piled on the little defenceman as if he had scored the Stanley Cup winning goal in overtime. In any other circumstance, this would have been a delay-of-game penalty for Brisbane, but the referee let it go. Even Muck was hammering the boards in admiration, cheering on the very team he was playing against.

After that, the game dramatically improved. Brisbane seemed to find their nerve playing the big team from Canada, the land of hockey, and they scored twice more to tie the game.

Nish scored on a rather overly dramatic rush from back of his own net, fell after he'd slipped the puck in, and lay on the ice, waiting for the Owls to leave the bench and pile on. But Muck, of course, would have nothing to do with such a display. Eventually Andy skated over and rapped his stick on Nish's knee pad, and Nish, beet-red even behind his mask, got slowly to his feet and skated back to the bench. They were laughing when he arrived, and he flung his stick down so hard it bounced off the first-aid kit and caught Mr. Dillinger on the arm.

"Far end," Muck told him.

It was all he needed to say. Nish moved down

and took his familiar "benched" seat at the far end. He had played his last shift against the Bandits.

They played another twenty minutes. Travis scored on a nifty backhander, and the Bandits scored again.

In the final minute, the Bandits coach brought his goalie out as an extra attacker, and Muck answered by bringing his goalie out as well. Travis had never heard of such a thing, but he guessed it wasn't against the rules. Muck also put out the Owls' weakest players, with instructions to take it easy.

Ten seconds to go, and the little defenceman who'd scored the Bandits' first goal got a backhand on a puck that was rolling up on its edge and lobbed it hard and high down the ice. It seemed, for a moment, as if the puck might lodge in the rafters, but it came down, bounced sharp to the right, skidded, and slid, and barely nipped into the near corner of the net.

Tie game!

The buzzer sounded and both sides cleared their benches, rushing out of habit to congratulate the goalies – only this time there were no goalies on the ice.

"Ridiculous!" Nish said as he skated out, pretending to be working out kinks and stiffness from sitting so long. "Muck had no reason to pull our goalie, as well."

"He wanted a tie game," said Travis.

"You know what they say in the NHL," Nish said.

"What?"

"A tie is like kissing your sister."

Travis turned, blinking in astonishment. "What's *that* supposed to mean?"

"It means ties suck, ties are for losers, ties don't mean anything, ties are like a 50 on your report card – you passed, but your mom's mad at you and your teacher never wants to see you again."

"You'd know about that!" Travis laughed.

The Brisbane Bandits weren't taking it like a 50 on a report card. A 5–5 tie against this top peewee hockey team from Canada was, Travis thought, more like an A+, like skipping a grade, like an extra month of summer holidays.

Or would it be "winter" holidays in Australia?

14

AFTER THE GAME, THE SCREECH OWLS TOOK THE train back out to the Olympic Park, where all the teams from the Oz Invitatonal had been given a full afternoon for practice.

It was beginning to sink in that the real joy of this tournament was going to be the Mini-Olympics. They'd had a good time playing the Bandits, and the Bandits had taken inspiration from their incredible tie game, but Muck had just proved that no matter how it was arranged, a competitive game was still more fun to play than a lopsided one.

The Mini-Olympics would be the real competition. Travis could sense it. The air was electric at the Olympic Park, the same high-tension, thrilling charge Travis normally felt at a top-rated hockey tournament. Everywhere they went there were competitors their own age working out and clocking themselves and trying to lift weights and hitting tennis balls and swimming and diving and dribbling basketballs. Just as the Owls – the visiting star team – felt a special glow whenever they took to the ice in Sydney, the Aussie kids took on their own glow when they appeared on the track and in the pool and on the basketball courts.

The Wizard of Oz could easily have got his nickname from playing a half dozen different sports. He was, Travis realized, a natural athlete. He could run faster than anyone else. He could swim faster. He could come within a few inches of actually dunking a basketball.

Everywhere Wiz went, Sarah could be found. Or was it the other way around? They had become a sort of golden couple of the Mini-Olympics – Sarah the best female athlete in the entire Olympic Park, Wiz the best male.

Nish was out of sorts. He was a star at hockey. He could be something of a star at lacrosse, as well. But Travis had never known Nish to play, or even care about, a single other sport.

Nish swam, but not very well. He was strong, but not nearly as strong as Sam or Andy or Wilson. He was so slow on the track he wouldn't even consider running.

"Why don't they make Nintendo an Olympic sport?" Nish whined.

"Well, it's not," Travis said.

"Or burping? Or making your armpits fart? Something I'm good at?"

"You're out of luck," said Travis.

"Or," Nish's eyes suddenly lit up, "why not skinny-dipping as an Olympic event?"

Travis's mind recoiled with an image of a

packed Olympic pool reacting in horror as Nish, butt-naked, raced in the doors and along the side of the pool and off the diving board – Nish, butt-naked at attention, the gold medal for Individual Skinny-Dipping around his neck while the Canadian flag was raised and "O Canada" struck up by the band, a small tear rolling down his cheek and off, bouncing off his shoulder to land on his other cheek. . . .

Travis shook off the thought. "Don't even think about it," he warned his unpredictable friend.

"Well," Nish moaned, "I gotta do *something*."

"You can practise our dives!" Sam interrupted.

"I can't dive from the tower!"

"You promised," Sam reminded him. "I put us down. We're on the list. You can't back out now – unless, of course, you're chicken."

Travis tried the 200-metre run and then the 400 metres – he liked the second distance better, not too short and not too long, a good test – and after he'd warmed down he decided to check out Nish and Sam's practice for synchronized diving.

A crowd had gathered at the pool. They were watching Wiz and Sarah race for fun – Wiz barely winning over eight lengths – and they were watching Liz and Sam practising their diving.

Sam noticed Travis coming in and waved to him from the top of the tower. She pointed down to the floor below her, and there Travis found Nish, huddled against the rail.

"You don't have to do it," Travis told him.

"Of course I have to. She dared."

"A dare doesn't mean a thing."

"Maybe not to you, pal. It means *everything* to me."

There was no use arguing. Nish was the only human being Travis knew who came complete with buttons. You couldn't see them, but they were there. Sarah knew exactly how to push them to get the reaction she wanted. Muck knew how to push them when he needed a good game. Sam was fast learning how to push them, too.

"You ready, Big Boy?" Sam called down.

Nish nodded. Sam dived, a perfect one-and-a-half somersault before she cut neatly into the water. She surfaced, pushing her hair back, and smiled up at Travis and Nish.

"We're going to win gold, you know – Nish 'n' me."

"I'll believe it when I see it," said Travis.

They began on the one-metre boards. With Sam advising, Nish dove again and again and again. She counted out "*one-two-three*" and then they both bounced and tried to leave their boards at the same time.

It took a while, but Nish was a fast learner. He might have a large body, but he had great control over it, and it didn't take him long to perfect the somersault and back dive and even a small twist. The more they dove, the more coordinated they became. Some of the dives were horrible, and everyone watching laughed mercilessly, but an increasing number were perfectly in time. A few times they dove so perfectly in tandem the pool erupted in a smattering of admiring applause.

"You're a natural, Big Boy!" Sam shouted.

Nish said nothing. He nodded. He didn't seem even remotely comfortable.

They moved to the three-metre boards, and Nish looked, for a moment, terrified. But Sam cajoled and prodded and coaxed, and eventually he began diving from the three-metre with the same surprising grace he'd shown on the one-metre.

"*We're headed for the gold medal!*" Sam shouted, pumping a fist after one perfectly matched dive.

It was time to try the tower. Sam went up first, and stopped at the first platform to wait for Nish.

Nish mounted the steps like a convicted murderer brought to a scaffold. He moved like a sloth, both hands firmly on the handrails, his feet so reluctant to leave the steps it seemed they might be glued there.

He made it to the first level and froze. Nothing Sam could say or do could convince him to climb higher. He stayed there, eyes closed, his entire body shaking.

"Travis!" Sam called. "You better come and help him down!"

Travis scrambled up the steps and took hold of Nish's wrist. His fingers were locked solid.

"Let go," Travis said. "We're going back down."

"I . . . can't . . . move," Nish said.

"You can't stay here."

"Keep your eyes shut," Sam said, "and we'll guide you."

Slowly, they brought Nish back down. There were a few giggles from the crowd, but no open laughter. It was one thing to kid Nish about his stupid ideas, but no one wanted to humiliate him.

As soon as Nish's feet touched the floor he opened his eyes – they were brimmed red, but perhaps that was just the chlorine in the pool.

He didn't say a word. He headed straight for the door and was out, gone.

"There goes my gold medal," sighed Sam.

15

MOST OF THE SCREECH OWLS WERE RELAXING IN a small park near their hotel. It was another warm, beautiful day. They had shopped for souvenirs along Harrington and Argyle – Nish bought his traditional tournament T-shirt, this one with a kangaroo with a pouch full of ice and cold beer – and they'd all bought ice-cream cones to eat while they sat about on the iron benches.

"Well," Sam said with a snicker, "would you look at that?"

Wiz and Sarah were walking towards them, hand in hand. Sam whistled loudly. Sarah let Wiz's hand drop. She obviously hadn't expected to run into her teammates.

"Where'd you get the ice cream?" Sarah asked as they came closer. Her face was pink.

"It'd melt before you two got within a mile of it," Liz giggled. Everyone else laughed. Wiz and Sarah looked embarrassed.

"We walked over to the aquarium," Sarah said.

"Find out anything?" Andy asked, licking the drops away from the bottom of his cone.

Everyone gathered around to get the news.

"The Great White has been let go," Sarah said. "They just wanted to be sure it was all right. It's fine, so they took it out to sea and released it."

"Won't the police need it for evidence?" Fahd asked.

"Not really," said Sarah. "They know it swallowed just the head without the rest of the body."

"Apart from that, the police aren't saying anything," said Wiz. "But one of the marine scientists at the aquarium told us they think it was an execution."

"*An execution!*" shouted Sam.

"That's right," Wiz said, lifting his right hand and chopping the air. "Someone probably sliced it off with a machete. He was probably on his knees with his hands behind his back when it happened."

"I'M GONNA HURL!" groaned Sam.

"That's my job," corrected Nish.

"But why?" Wilson repeated. "Did they have any thoughts on why?"

Sarah and Wiz shook their heads. "They don't know," said Wiz. "They figure it must have happened at sea. I mean that's pretty obvious, isn't it? The shark didn't crawl up on a beach somewhere and gobble down the head. It probably happened in a boat. But only the person who did it knows where, and why."

"Creepy," said Jenny.

"We also talked to someone there about

traditional Chinese medicines," Sarah said. "She knew everything about seahorses and why they're considered such powerful medicine. She says hardly anyone knows much about the seadragons, though, only that they're considered to have even stronger powers."

"She found out we were in the Mini-Olympics," laughed Wiz, "and you wouldn't believe the things some of the athletes did at the Olympic Games."

"Like what?" Wilson pressed.

"Like drinking the stomach contents of honey bees," Sarah said, laughing.

"*Disgusting!*" shouted Liz.

"If you think that's bad, how about injecting your veins with spider blood?" Wiz said. "That's what the Chinese swimmers said gave them so much energy."

"That's crazy!" said Fahd. "It makes no sense."

"Hey," Wiz interrupted. "They won gold medals, didn't they? They're the best in the world, aren't they?"

Nish was listening intently. His eyes were wide open and he was nodding up and down. Normally, he would have been the first to make a joke about spider blood or bee vomit, but instead he looked like he was sitting in a church pew nodding in agreement to a sermon.

What, Travis asked himself, *could Nish possibly be thinking?*

16

THE SCREECH OWLS WERE UP FOR ANOTHER game in the Oz Invitational, this time against the Perth Pirates. They went ahead 6–0 in the first period on two goals by Jesse Highboy, a break-away marker by Simon Milliken, and a goal each by the Travis–Sarah–Dmitri line.

At the break, Muck called Sarah and Travis aside and told them to take off their sweaters and follow Mr. Dillinger. Mr. Dillinger led them to the Pirates' dressing room and knocked on the door. The Pirates' manager opened it, welcomed them with a big "G'day, mates!" and tossed a couple of fresh sweaters their direction.

"You can join your mate around the corner – we cleared some space for the three of you."

Sarah, a half step ahead of Travis, suddenly pumped a fist in the air and shouted. "*Yes!*"

Someone else was also pulling on a Pirates sweater.

Wiz!

He pulled his head through the neck hole, shook his curls, and grinned at them. "I made a special request for my old linemates," he laughed.

Three of the Pirates' weaker players were already off to join the Owls. The coaches were mixing things up a bit again. Wiz had been invited down out of the stands, where he and some of the Sharks had come to watch the Owls play, and with the addition of Travis and Sarah the Pirates would have one line better than anything the Owls could put on the ice.

Now they had a game going.

The Pirates came to life thanks to the new line. Wiz, teamed up once more with players equal to his extraordinary talents, was getting better and better every shift. He made miraculous passes to Sarah and Travis, and always seemed to be in position whenever one of them ended up with the puck in a corner of the Pirates' end.

Wiz scored twice on hard one-timers after being set up in the slot. Sarah scored a beautiful goal on an end-to-end rush. Travis scored on a pretty tic-tac-toe play in which Sarah left a drop pass for Wiz coming in late, who worked a perfect spinnerama around the Pirates defence before rapping a backhand pass to Travis on the open side.

They were within two goals of the Owls when Wiz picked up the puck in his own end and flew the full length of the ice with only Nish scrambling back in time. Wiz came in over the Owls' blueline, dropped the puck into his skates, and tried, once again, the spinning move that had worked so perfectly only minutes before.

This time, however, Nish was ready for him.

Nish stepped forward, bringing his gloves up into Wiz's face, and he flattened the Australian so hard Travis could hear the crack against the ice two lines away.

Wiz spun into the corner, his body limp.

Nish picked up the puck, ignoring the referee's whistle, and slapped it all the way down the ice.

The whistle went again.

Suddenly everyone was shoving. Travis had been in shoving matches before, but usually in defence of his silly friend. This time it was Travis shoving Nish, and Sarah coming in screaming at him.

"What was *that* all about?" she shouted.

Her face was red with anger. Nish's face was redder yet. He looked like a tomato about to explode.

"*He's a hot dog!*" Nish shouted back, shaking off Travis's grip.

"Who are you to call anyone a hot dog!" Sarah yelled, her voice shaking.

Wiz, who was now up on one knee in the corner, looked more puzzled than shocked. Travis figured it was probably the first time anyone had ever taken a run at him. From what he'd seen of Wiz's talents, though, it wouldn't be the last.

"*Bug off!*" Nish snarled, shaking everyone off and skating away to take his rightful place in the penalty box.

Sarah skated towards Wiz, now trying to get on his feet.

He wobbled slightly, his legs suddenly rubber.

"You better get to the bench," said Sarah.

"I'm okay," Wiz said, but he slipped and almost fell again.

Sarah took one side and Travis the other, and they skated him back to the bench, where the manager and coach reached out and helped him to a seat.

Wiz was smiling.

Travis had never seen such a reaction. In any other hockey game he'd ever been in where something stupid like this had happened, the anger would last through the rest of the game and sometimes into the next. There'd be bad feelings and talk of revenge.

"I guess I was asking for that," Wiz said. "Tell your mate I owe him one, okay, Trav?"

Travis nodded. He would certainly do that. Nish deserved whatever was coming to him.

After Nish had served his penalty, Muck sent him to the far end of the bench to sit in a spot all too familiar to him – hockey's equivalent to the desk in the far corner of the classroom.

Wiz took one more shift but was still a little unsteady from the hit and skated off early. He didn't return for another shift.

The game never regained its energy. Fahd scored on a point shot that hit a defenceman's skate and went in. Wilson scored on a long shot that bounced once and skittered between the goalie's pads. Travis scored a second on a nice breakaway pass from Sarah. Dmitri scored on his customary high backhand. Sarah set up their new winger, probably the quickest of the Pirates, for a breakaway, and he scored when he fanned on the shot.

The Owls won 9–6, but the Pirates acted as if they, in fact, had won the entire tournament. Never before had they scored so many goals – even if five of the six had come from players "on loan" to them – and they seemed delighted merely to be on the same ice surface as such skilled players from Canada and the legendary Wizard of Oz from Sydney. Several of the players even insisted on getting their photos taken with Sarah and Travis before they took off their equipment.

One of the Pirates, the quick little player who'd scored on the fanned shot, said he'd see them again in the Mini-Olympics. "We're a lot better at those sports than we are at this one, y'know," he told them.

Travis was beginning to suspect that they all were – that the Mini-Olympics were going to be the great equalizer for the Owls.

17

DATA PICKED UP A COPY OF THE *HERALD* ON their way back to the hotel. There was a photograph of the shark that had been released by the aquarium, and an update on the mysterious head that had been burped up by the huge fish.

"He's a Filipino!" Data announced after he had scanned the article.

"How can they tell?" Fahd asked.

"Maybe that's where his shoes were made," offered Nish.

"Save your sick jokes for your friends," Sarah advised. "If you have any left."

Travis couldn't help notice that Sarah still hadn't forgiven Nish for his hit on Wiz.

Nish was in trouble with his whole team, not just Sarah. Travis had told him that Wiz had said he "owed him one," but Nish had just laughed it off as if the whole thing was no big deal.

Data laid the paper open on his lap and gave the Owls the essence of the article.

"Dental analysis," he said. "Something about the type of filling material only being available in the Philippines, anyway."

"Great," said Wilson. "Only eighty million dental records to check."

"It's a start," Data argued.

"Why don't they just look for a body that's missing a head?" Nish suggested.

●

There was a sharp rap at the door.

Travis, who'd been lying on his bed half watching television while Nish and Fahd napped, jumped up and went quickly to the peephole.

It was Andy, a look of concern on his face.

Travis opened the door to let him in, but Andy had other ideas. He wanted Travis to come with him. "Data's been on the Internet again," he said. "Says he thinks he might have found something."

Data was deep in thought when they walked in, staring at the screen of his laptop as if it held some enormous secret he could not quite read.

He turned his chair when he heard the door click. "Hi, Trav," he said. "I've been doing some research for us. Did you know the number-one research spot for seahorses is in Canada? Project Seahorse, at McGill University in Montreal."

Travis shook his head. Of course he didn't know.

"Project Seahorse has links to everyone. They've even funded an experiment with fishermen in the Philippines to see if they can build a seahorse fishery that's sustainable."

Travis wondered when Data was going to get to the interesting part. But he said nothing.

"The Philippines is where almost all seahorse fishermen come from," Data continued. He clicked the mouse and a page from a scientific article popped up. "The average income in those villages is around three hundred dollars," he read. "That's for an entire year. Can you imagine?"

"I get almost that for my allowance," said Andy.

Travis shook his head. It was exactly the amount of money he'd brought on this trip, and he'd been planning to spend every penny before leaving. He felt a little guilty that a person might make no more than that in an entire year – and be expected to feed a family on it.

"That's the huge attraction of seahorse harvesting," Data continued. "Remember that bowl of seahorse soup Fahd found on the Internet – four hundred and fifty dollars for just one bowl in Taiwan?"

Travis nodded. He remembered.

"And a kilogram of dried seahorses being worth as much as fifteen thousand dollars?"

Travis nodded again.

"That's why there's such a big concern about the future of seahorses. Already one species on the endangered list and several others in trouble. Areas that used to produce lots of seahorses are now fished out around the Philippines, and now there are press reports about Philippine fishermen in Australian waters after seahorses – apparently it's becoming a major political issue."

Travis could no longer help himself. "So?"

"So," Data said slowly, as if explaining to a very dull student, "if seahorses are that valuable, what must a seadragon be worth?"

Travis half followed, but still couldn't figure out exactly where Data was headed.

"Did you get a good look at that guy who attacked Nish?" Data asked.

Travis shook his head. "I didn't see much."

"Anything?" Data asked. "Eyes? Colour of hair? Anything at all."

"Black," Travis answered after he thought about it. "He had black hair. Thick and fairly long. It was flowing when they fought."

Data clicked through a few more pages. Travis waited for him to say more, but Data seemed deep in thought.

"What?" Travis finally asked.

"Remember Wiz saying the head had been sliced off by a machete?"

"Yeah."

"Well, that suggests he was executed. The police have said he was Filipino. Maybe he was poaching around that island and maybe the guy who attacked Nish – or the gang that guy belonged to – decided they wanted him out of there so they could have all the seadragons to themselves."

"I don't know," said Travis.

"How much do you think that sack of sea-dragons he had weighed?"

Travis had no idea. They'd immediately let go the ones that were still alive, and they'd thrown overboard the ones that were dead – except, of course, for the one that Sarah had so carefully saved and that was now dried out on a dresser in the room Sarah was sharing with Liz, Sam, and Jenny.

"Wet or dry?" Travis asked. He'd noted there was quite a difference after being allowed to examine Sarah's treasure.

"Dried," Data said.

"I don't know. A couple of pounds, at least. More than a kilo."

Data gave a very slight nod of satisfaction. "Seahorses at fifteen thousand dollars a kilogram," he said slowly. "Think how much a kilogram of seadragons would be worth to a poor fisherman."

Travis tried.

He could imagine the money. He could not, however, imagine it being worth taking a machete and lopping off a person's head.

Nothing could be worth that.

18

SARAH AND WIZ WENT BACK TO THE AQUARIUM to see if they could find out where, exactly, the Great White Shark had been caught up in the fishing nets.

They came back an hour later. Their new friends had been helpful, but no one kept records like that. All the aquarium staff had was a phone number for the captain of the fishing boat that had brought the shark in. Sarah and Wiz had been able to reach him straight away, but he wasn't exactly helpful. He figured it had been in the direction of the island they were thinking of, but he pointed out with a laugh, "Sharks swim around, you know. The Pacific Ocean is a bit bigger than a holding tank at the Sydney Aquarium."

"The direction is right," said Data, who was convinced there was a connection. "Let's say they executed him the same day the shark got caught. The head hadn't been digested at all. We can *presume* the shark was at least in the vicinity of the island around that time. And we know that the seadragons are found there."

"Circumstantial evidence," said Sam. "The police would laugh in your face."

"We need more," Data said. "What about the video Wiz's mother took?"

"You can barely make it out," said Sarah. "It was shot into the sun. You can't make out anything on the boat. No name, nothing. You can barely see what shape it is. There's no flag – so we have no idea where they came from."

"What about going back?" Data asked.

"How?" Andy wondered.

"What about Wiz?" Data said. "Maybe he could ask his father?"

Somehow, Wiz had talked his father into doing it. With Sarah and Travis's help, he laid out all the evidence that the Owls had gathered – no matter how questionable it was – and asked him simply to take them back out to the island the following morning with the video camera. If the seadragon fishermen weren't there, then they'd have to admit they were beat.

Mr. Roberts had understood. He wasn't convinced there was any connection between the head and the seadragons, but he *was* convinced that his son would never forgive him if he didn't at least try.

They met at the Mosman Bay marina shortly after breakfast. They were a smaller group this time, just Mr. Roberts, Wiz, Sarah, Travis, and Nish. Travis had worked hard to convince Nish to come. He hoped Nish might apologize to Wiz so that they could make up, but it seemed that Nish agreed to come only because he had nothing else to do.

Wiz had said nothing. He'd never mentioned the hit again. Travis envied him his endlessly sunny disposition.

The seas were as calm as they had been the first day. Mr. Roberts ran at three-quarters throttle, the sleek boat clipping over the low waves in a steady machine-gun chop that cut down on the rolling and made Travis feel sleepy. He slouched down in the sun, spread on some sunscreen, and let himself doze off.

He woke up only when he sensed the engines being cut. It took several moments for his eyes to adjust to the brightness. He blinked, and blinked again. The boat was settling, rolling and rocking as it slowed. Off in the distance he could make out the island.

Mr. Roberts had the binoculars up to his eyes. He was scanning the seas on all sides. Travis was certain he had seen something when Mr. Roberts suddenly held the binoculars steady and adjusted the focus.

He handed them to Wiz. "About two o'clock," Mr. Roberts said.

Wiz looped the strap around his own neck and stared off in the direction of the 2 on a clock face.

"There's something there all right," he said after a while.

They all took turns looking. When Travis got the binoculars, it took him several moments to settle on a glimmering white object that seemed to bob and wink in the swells. It was much too far, even with the powerful binoculars, for him to make out anything on the boat. He couldn't even tell if there were any people on deck.

"Can we get closer?" Wiz asked.

"Not without them seeing us," said Mr. Roberts.

"But we need a photograph," Sarah added.

Mr. Roberts nodded. "You'd get nothing from here, even with the zoom," he said. "We've got to get closer – but we have to do it without alerting them."

"How?" asked Wiz.

Mr. Roberts smiled. "Simple. We run right at 'em full throttle. By the time they see us, we'll have your shot. Okay?"

Sarah shrieked. "*Okay!*"

"*Let's do it!*" shouted Wiz.

"Get the camera ready," Mr. Roberts said. "*And hang on for your life!*"

The big boat shuddered, reared like a horse, and bolted straight into the coming waves. As it gathered speed it rose gradually until they were planing over the waves, heading straight for the unknown boat.

Travis felt the deck shudder. He grabbed onto the handrail, the wind whipping his face as he stared straight ahead.

Nish clung to the boat's antenna, which was bolted to the port side of the cabin area. He held fast, his flesh jiggling as the boat clipped hard over the water. Travis could barely see Nish's face. He could see enough, however, to know that Nish was not liking this. Not liking it at all.

Up ahead, staring straight into the wind, Wiz and Sarah hung partly onto the railing, partly onto each other.

Mr. Roberts pushed the engine to full throttle, the boat roaring loudly as it seemed to rise even higher, all but flying over the low swells.

The strange boat was fast coming into view. It was difficult to tell – they would have to compare when they got home – but it looked like the one on Mrs. Roberts' video.

Sarah had the camera. She was trying to steady herself and focus ahead on the boat, which now seemed to be rushing towards them.

Something moved on the deck!

It was a man, and he was throwing scuba equipment into a hold. Another man emerged from the tiny cabin, stared towards them, then drew his head back in.

The water began to churn at the stern of the boat, the engines firing in a cloud of blue smoke.

"*They're running!*" Wiz called from the bow.

Travis took a quick glance at Nish. He was green, his eyes squeezed shut and his mouth in a painful grimace. He looked like he was about to be sick.

The first man on the unknown boat now ran to a wooden box on deck, reached in, and pulled out something long and dark.

"*Get down!*" Mr. Roberts yelled. "*He's got a gun!*"

Mr. Roberts turned the boat sharply, sending Travis spilling across the deck. He caught himself and looked quickly back to where Nish had been.

He was still there, glued to the antenna, his eyes still shut! Travis suddenly realized how dangerously exposed his friend was.

The man levelled the gun at the approaching boat.

"*NISH!*"

The voice belonged to Wiz.

Wiz left Sarah, who was still taking pictures, and ran towards the antenna. He dove before he got to Nish, knocking him away from the antenna and down onto the deck, and landing hard on top!

KRRRRACK!

SSSSSMACK!

The two sounds were almost simultaneous.

The first came from the boat just ahead of them. The second came from Mr. Roberts's antenna.

Travis turned just in time to see the antenna crash down over the railing and break off into the sea. The shot had struck it exactly where Nish had been clinging.

"*Hang on!*" Mr. Roberts yelled.

KRRRRACK!

Another shot, but not nearly so close.

KRRRRACK!

Again, but still farther away.

Mr. Roberts had the boat turned right around now and was racing back hard in the direction they had come.

Travis chanced a look over the railing. The other boat wasn't following. They were free.

He heard a groan and knew it was Nish.

Had he been hit?

But there was no blood. Wiz was carefully disentangling himself from Nish, who was twisting and moaning on the deck. Wiz grabbed Nish's hand and pulled him to a sitting position.

"What hit me?" Nish asked.

"It's what *didn't* hit you that you should be thinking about," Wiz said, laughing.

Nish shook his head, still not understanding.

He turned and looked back at the shattered antenna.

Exactly where he would have been standing, if Wiz hadn't taken him out.

Nish looked over at Wiz, his mouth moving helplessly.

Wiz smiled. "Hey," he said. "I owed you one – remember?"

Sarah hurried over, breathless. She was holding the camera as if she were afraid it might break, or vanish.

"I got some great shots!" she said.

Wiz laughed. "Thank God *they* didn't or we'd be one Nish short right about now!"

Nish shook his head and stared at Wiz.

He still didn't know what had just happened.

19

THEY RETURNED TO MOSMAN BAY WITH NO trouble. The mystery boat had not given chase, and Mr. Roberts, fortunately, knew the sea and shoreline so well he was able to find his way back even though the antenna was useless.

They'd turned over Data's theories and Sarah's photographs to the Coast Guard and told them about being fired on by the mysterious fishing boat. The Coast Guard promised they'd look into the matter immediately.

There was nothing else for the Owls to do. There was no point in just waiting around to see what the Coast Guard could find out. It might take days.

Besides, the Games were about to begin.

As soon as they were off the ice, the Screech Owls became the underdogs.

Whoever had set up the Mini-Olympics had done a wonderful job. There were roughly ten Australians for every Screech Owl, but everything was evened out by turning the first six places in each event into points, and multiplying by ten each time a Screech Owl placed in the top six.

Fahd took silver in archery. Sarah took a gold in the 200-metre, a silver in the long jump, and a bronze in both the high jump and the hurdles. Wilson took a silver in weightlifting. Derek and Jesse came fourth in tennis doubles. Andy took bronze in the javelin, and Simon took a bronze in wrestling. Travis came fourth in the 400-metre and fifth in the pole vault, an event he'd never even tried until this day.

The best story, however, was in the pool, where Sarah and Wiz seemed to be stepping onto the podium every few minutes. Wiz was a wonderful swimmer, and took three golds in different events. Sarah took two golds and a silver. Liz took a silver and a gold in the butterfly – the only Owl who could do the difficult stroke – and Jesse came fifth in the backstroke.

The final scheduled event of the day was diving. Players, parents, and competitors packed into the Olympic pool for the windup to what had already been a wonderful day. Two Aussies – a girl from Melbourne, and a teammate of Wiz's on the Sydney Sharks – dominated the events and took the top medals. Sam, diving in the individual events, took a silver and a bronze, and Sarah took a fourth in the one-metre competition.

Just before the synchronized diving event, the organizers called a time out.

"Just thought you might all like to know the running tally," a man wearing an Australian team tracksuit said over the public address system. "With the scores weighted to take into consideration our special visitors from Canada, we have the day's standings at Australia 211, Canada 209."

A huge cheer went up from the mostly Australian crowd.

"Can you believe it?" Sarah said, turning with her hands pressed to the side of her face. "We're almost tied."

"Down to the final event," Muck chuckled. "Sudden death overtime in the Olympics."

"But, but," Sam sputtered, "we only entered synchronized diving as a joke!"

"Well," said Mr. Dillinger. "Looks like the joke's on us, then. Which reminds me. Where is our other diver?"

Everyone looked around for Nish.

"He went back to the hotel around noon," Andy said.

Sarah looked stricken. "He wouldn't bail on us?"

"Sure he would," said Sam, shaking her head. "He's chicken – we all know that."

"I saw him a few minutes ago at the snack bar!" Fahd announced.

"*He's here?*" Sam shouted.

Travis jumped in. "I'll get him," he said to Sam. "You get ready."

Travis ran up through the stands, and into the corridor where the snack bars were located. He turned right, then left, following his instincts: the fancier snack bar was to the left. He ran down the corridor, past parents and young hockey players who were happily buying up souvenirs and waiting in line for ice-cream bars. Down around the corner and towards the far exit he ran, hoping, praying, that Nish would be there. The Screech Owls' Olympic hopes lay with him.

It seemed ridiculous to Travis. None of the Owls had taken the Mini-Olympics very seriously, believing that, on average, the Australian kids would be far superior to them at almost anything but hockey. But no one could have predicted how dominant Sarah would be in her events – inspired, no doubt, by Wiz's equally impressive performance. No one could have predicted that all the Owls would get so caught up in the competition. And now it was all down to one event that they had considered little more than a joke.

Nish, with his great fear of heights, diving from the high tower.

Travis turned the corner and could see the large snack bar in the distance. A bulky body was sitting at one of the tables, his back to Travis, but unmistakable all the same.

"Nish!" Travis called as he flew into the snack bar so fast his sneakers skidded and squeaked on the floor. "You're on! You're up! They're calling the diving event."

Nish appeared completely calm, but he had a disgusted look on his face. He was sitting before a bowl of soup, a small plastic bag on the table to one side, and he was slowly spooning the remainder of the soup into his mouth.

How can he eat at a time like this? Travis wondered.

"Just give me another minute," Nish said.

Travis sat, waiting, while Nish carefully finished off his soup, pulling a face for every spoonful.

"If it tastes so awful," Travis asked, "why finish it?"

Nish grimaced. "Always clean up your plate, Travis. Didn't your mother teach you any manners?"

Travis shook his head. A lecture on good manners from Wayne Nishikawa was the last thing in the world he ever expected to hear.

"Hurry up!" Travis urged.

Nish tilted the bowl, filled the spoon, and slotted it into his mouth, swallowing quickly.

He burped and set the spoon down.

"You'll have to run!" Travis warned.

Nish looked at him, then down at his table. "Clean this up for me, then," he said. "I'll go ahead."

"Sure, sure – whatever. Just hurry!"

Nish pushed himself up, the chair growling across the polished concrete, and began hurrying off in the direction Travis had come from. Travis gathered up the bowl and spoon and tray and began heading for the garbage can.

He'd forgotten the plastic bag.

He stepped back and grabbed it. It felt empty, except there was the sound of fine grains of salt or sand running inside.

He set the tray down, opened the bag, and peered in.

Whatever it was, it was very dry, and flaky.

He sniffed at the bag.

He knew that smell!

The ocean . . . the smell on the boat . . . a fishy smell . . .

Nish hadn't!

He couldn't have!

Travis sniffed again, his mind racing. There was no doubt about it. He recognized the smell now.

The seadragon. Sarah's dried-out seadragon. The little creature with the mythical ability to give a man courage.

Sarah's seadragon ground into powder and mixed in a soup.

And now in the stomach of Wayne Nishikawa, *tower diver.*

20

SAM WAS ALREADY WAITING AT THE TOWER WHEN
Travis arrived back at the pool. She and everyone
else seemed to be looking at exactly the same place:
the doorway to the showers and change rooms.

Ten seconds later, the doors opened.

It was Nish, in his Mighty Ducks of Anaheim
bathing trunks. He raised both arms to the crowd
like he was the wrestling heavyweight champion
of the world.

The stands erupted in cheers.

Nish bowed.

He's going to make a fool of himself, Travis
thought. *He's going to panic.*

The Australian synchronized diving team was
already at the top of the tower. It struck Travis,
from the way they were joking around and laughing, that perhaps they had taken this particular
event no more seriously than had the Owls.
Surely, though, they hadn't entered any hockey
players who were terrified of heights.

The two Aussies moved to the edge, high
above the water, talked over their planned dive,

high-fived each other for luck, and leapt off at the count of three.

One flipped frontwards, the other managed only a half-flip, and they crashed heavily into the water, bodies badly out of time.

They surfaced to a loud chorus of good-natured booing from the Australian players in the stands.

Both waved, laughing.

Thank heavens, Travis thought. *They're not taking this seriously, either. But they'll still win*, he realized. *Because Nish won't even be able to climb up, let alone jump off – and the Mini-Olympic championship will be theirs.*

Nish was at the steps. He had one hand on the railing. Sam was just ahead of him, pleading with him to hurry. From the look on her face, she seemed a lot more agitated than Nish.

Nish smiled, turned and waved again, causing a ripple of laughter to move through the crowd.

He scurried up the steps to join Sam.

He must have his eyes closed, thought Travis. *This is where he froze last time.*

But Nish didn't freeze, he didn't even pause. He took Sam's hand as he reached her and almost hauled her up the next series of steps to the top of the tower.

The Owls gasped. Nish was now ten metres above the water. He was standing on a small platform four storeys high, with nothing but air between him and the water.

And he wasn't screaming!

He wasn't screaming. He wasn't crying. He didn't have his eyes shut. He wasn't shaking. And he wasn't hanging on to anything but Sam's hand while he waved with the other.

Sam looked as baffled as anyone else in the crowd. But she shrugged, turned to Nish, went over some quick instructions as to what they'd do, and the two of them approached the edge of the tower.

The entire pool took one breath and held it, as if they, not the divers, were about to plunge underwater.

In the eerie silence, everyone could hear Sam's soft voice doing the countdown.

"Three . . . two . . . one!"

At *"one!"* both left the tower. Nish held a swan dive, as did Sam, and then both, almost in perfect unison, did a quick flip before entering the water. The splash was so small it seemed more like two coins striking the water than two hockey players who'd never dived competitively in their lives.

A huge cheer went up from the crowd, the Aussies louder than the Canadians.

Sam and Nish surfaced, fists pumping.

"KAAA–WAAA–BUNGA!" they shouted together.

"KAAA–WAAA–BUNGA!" the crowd shouted back, laughing.

Twice more they dove, Nish each time racing fearlessly up the steps and onto the tower. They tried back dives that almost worked, and a double flip that worked remarkably well. The Australians pulled off a nearly perfect flip and twist, but their third dive might as well have been called "Cannonballs off the High Tower." They hit the water so hard, with such a huge splash, that the crowd gasped with relief just to see they were still alive.

"*The results of the synchronized diving event!*" the announcer's voice echoed throughout the large pool. "*Canada takes the gold medal!*"

The crowd, Aussies as well as Canadians, exploded in cheers.

Nish and Sam had won the gold.

The Canadians had won the Mini-Olympics!

It seemed impossible to Travis that it was over so soon. He had looked forward to the Mini-Olympics since they'd been announced, and now they were history.

The flag had been raised, the national anthem sung, the medals strung about Nish's and Sam's necks, and everyone in the crowd had congratulated each other on such a marvellous day. Travis's back had been slapped until it burned. Wiz had given him a hug so hard he thought his ribs would break – though it seemed like half the hug Wiz had reserved for Sarah.

Everyone was asking to see Nish's medal. He had it off his neck now and was handing it about, when suddenly he stepped back from the gathering of well-wishers.

How unlike Nish, Travis thought. *He's finally got exactly what he wants, why wouldn't he revel in it?*

But then he got a better look at his friend. Nish was a little green about the gills again.

"You okay?" Travis asked his friend.

Nish burped lightly. "I don't feel so good."

"Something you ate?" Travis asked, grinning.

Nish looked hard at him, eyes narrowing. "Who told you?"

Travis shook his head. "Who's going to tell Sarah?"

"What do you mean?"

"She wanted to keep that seadragon, don't you think?"

But whatever Nish was thinking, it had nothing to do with what Sarah wanted or not. He was very green now.

He put his hand over his mouth.

With his other hand, he pushed Travis aside, running hard for the washroom.

21

THERE WAS MUCH LAUGHTER AND SHOUTING ON the train ride back to the hotel. Nish and Sam were cheered, and Fahd returned Nish's treasured gold medal to its rightful owner. Travis told the story of the plastic bag and the funny smell and how he'd finally figured out that Nish had powdered up the dried seadragon and eaten it with soup to give him the "courage" he lacked. And who could now argue that it was just a silly myth? It had worked, hadn't it?

"How much did you say a bowl of that soup cost?" Sarah asked Data.

"In Taiwan, four hundred and fifty dollars."

"Well, then, that's what Nish owes me, I guess," she said.

"That's nothing compared to what you all owe me!" protested Nish, only to be drowned out by happy boos.

When they finally got back to the hotel, Mr. Dillinger and Muck had them all gather in the lobby. There was news, and Muck wanted them all to hear it.

Mr. Roberts was there with a uniformed member of the Coast Guard.

"This is Captain Peterkin," Mr. Roberts said. The Coast Guard captain nodded. "They've made a series of arrests today and would like to talk to you."

Captain Peterkin cleared his throat. He had a finely clipped, sand-coloured beard, and a large moustache that wiggled oddly as he spoke. Some of the Owls fought off giggles as he began speaking, but when they realized what it was he was saying, they all grew quiet.

"The man whose head was discovered at the Sydney Aquarium," the Coast Guard officer said, "has been identified as a Filipino fisherman who was illegally trapping seadragons off the south coast of Australia, mostly in an area just off Sydney Harbour."

"How was he killed?" asked Fahd.

Captain Peterkin cleared his throat again. "Executed, we believe," he said. "Several different poaching operations were competing for the same ripe area for seadragons. Thanks to photographic evidence produced by" – he consulted a small index card in his hand – "Miss Sarah Cuthbertson, we were able to make a positive ID on a Philippines fishing boat in our waters and conduct a stop and seizure operation. We found several kilograms of expired seadragons. We also seized a number of weapons, including a high-powered hunting rifle and several machetes."

"I thought so," said Fahd.

"We also have a confession from one of the apprehended fishermen. There had been a battle for these particular seadragon grounds, and, it seems, our unfortunate headless man was one of the losers."

Travis couldn't stop himself. He had to know. "I don't understand something," he said.

The Coast Guard captain raised one eyebrow in Travis's direction.

"Why would that man attack Nish? He must have been trying to kill him, but all he had to do was swim away and we'd probably never have noticed."

The Coast Guard captain looked around, puzzled.

"Which one of you is Nish?" he asked.

Nish stepped forward, blushing hard.

The captain looked a long time at him. Nish grew redder and redder. Finally the captain scratched his beard and nodded, satisfied.

"Put a diving mask on this young man," Captain Peterkin said, "and put him underwater, and you'd all probably mistake him for a Filipino poacher."

"Impossible," Nish said, a smile returning to his beaming face.

"And why's that, son?"

"Because I can't *stand* seadragons – that's why."

22

THERE WAS ONE FINAL HOCKEY GAME STILL TO play. It would be the *grand finale* of the Oz Invitational, the Screech Owls of Tamarack, Canada, against an all-star team of the best peewee hockey players in all of Australia. Wiz Roberts would captain the Aussie All-Stars against Travis Lindsay and the Screech Owls.

They played at the Macquarie Ice Rink, but so many curious spectators wanted to watch, they could almost have filled an Olympic stadium. The organizers packed in as many as could legally fit and then turned a blind eye as dozens more squeezed in. At 7:00 on a Saturday night they dropped the puck.

"*Dah, da-da-da, da-ahhhh!*" Nish sang as he lined up beside Travis before the anthems.

"Hockey Night in Australia?" Travis asked, smiling.

"You got it, *myte*," Nish answered in an Aussie accent.

This game was different. The two teams were perfectly balanced. Wiz was the equal of Sarah on the ice, and each of the Aussie teams in the tournament had one, two, or three youngsters good enough to play for the Screech Owls. And the Aussies were so fired up by the chance to play on an all-star team in front of such a loud, boisterous crowd that they all seemed faster, smarter, and bigger than before.

"These guys are good," Travis said on the bench after his first shift.

"They're amazing!" said Dmitri.

Travis and Sarah leaned back and winked at each other behind his back. It was great to be back with Dmitri. It had been fun playing with Wiz, but the three Owls had a special connection.

Dmitri scored the first goal on a play Travis had seen so many times it seemed he was watching an old movie. Sarah won a faceoff and got the puck back to Nish behind Jenny's net. Nish moved up towards the blueline and lifted the puck so high it almost hit the rafters. Dmitri, anticipating perfectly, chased the puck down when it landed and came in on a clear breakaway. Shoulder fake, shift to backhand, a high lifter – and the Aussie water bottle was in the air, saluting Dmitri's trademark move.

Travis realized that playing against Wiz was very different from playing with him. He was astonished at how strong he was on the puck; he simply refused to be knocked off. He scored once and set up a second, and halfway through the first period Muck countered by insisting

Travis's line go head-to-head with Wiz's line whenever the Aussie sensation was on the ice.

That meant Sarah against Wiz, Wiz against Sarah. They checked each other. They faced off against each other.

Travis wondered how they would handle this, but he had his answer almost at once when Sarah shouldered Wiz hard out of the faceoff circle and used her skate to kick the puck to Travis.

Travis curled back, losing his check. He looked up and down the ice. Lars was free on the far side, and he fired the puck back to him.

Lars took stock of the ice, faked a pass over to Wilson, and instead chopped the puck off the boards to Dmitri. Dmitri took off like a shot up the far wing and slipped a quick pass to Sarah, now hitting centre.

But the pass never got to her. Using his shoulder, Wiz easily knocked Sarah off the puck, grabbed it, and turned hard back the other way.

Lars and Wilson tried to take away his space by closing in on him, but Wiz saw it coming. He plucked the puck off the ice so it sailed between the two squeezing defenders and leapt into the air over them, Lars and Wilson crashing together in a tangle of sticks and skates.

Wiz was in alone. He deked out Jenny and fired the puck hard into the goal. He turned, laughing, and plucked the puck off the ice as it rebounded out of the net, twisting his stick perfectly so the puck lay on the blade, just like an NHLer, and handed it to the linesman.

Heading into the third period, the Owls were down 5–3. Muck, for the first time, seemed really into the game. He had his coach's face on, giving away nothing, but telling each and every one of the Owls that this was the time to get serious. No more shinny. No more glory plays. Just real *hockey*.

"Nothing stupid, Nishikawa," he said. "We need you on the ice, not in the penalty box."

Nish nodded and he stared straight down at his skate laces.

Nish is in the game, Travis told himself. *Nothing to worry about there.*

"We need you, Sarah," Muck said.

Sarah nodded, her face streaming with sweat. It would be up to her, both to hold off Wiz and to make sure the Owls came back.

The crowd had grown so loud Travis wondered if they were pumping in a tape of a Stanley Cup game. It seemed impossible that so few people could make so much noise. But they were all Aussies, he reminded himself, and there was no louder fan on earth than the Aussie at full volume.

Besides, they could sense a win. They could smell victory. To beat the Canadians at their own game would be something special.

Travis slapped his stick against Nish's shin pads before the faceoff. Nish never looked up. His face was as red as the helmets on the Aussie All-Stars. Sweat was rolling off him, and they hadn't even started the final period. He was in the Nish Zone – and Travis was glad to see him there.

Nish began the charge. He picked up a puck in his own end, faked a pass up to Travis, and carried out, playing a sweet give-and-go with Dmitri at centre ice.

Nish, carrying again, came across the Aussie blueline, tucked a drop pass between his legs, and left the puck for Sarah as he took out the one Aussie defender.

That left Sarah and Travis with a two-on-one. Sarah waited, faked a shot, and then slid a hard pass across the crease to Travis, standing at the corner of the net all alone.

It was one of the easiest goals of his life. He simply let the puck hit his stick and tick off into the net.

Nish would also set up the tying goal. He carried again, a few minutes later, and hit Andy with a long breakaway pass. Andy came in, rifled a slapshot off the post, and Nish, charging hard to the net, picked up the rebound and stuffed it before the goaltender could get across to block his shot.

Aussies 5, Owls 5.

With the clock ticking down, Wiz brought the crowd to its feet with a stupendous carry that began in his own end and involved stickhandling past Sarah not once, not twice, but three times.

But Sarah would not give up. She chased and chased, using her speed to cut off the twisting, turning Wiz as he worked his way up-ice.

At one point Travis could see Wiz laughing as Sarah slid in, once again, to knock the puck free. But with two blinding-fast hand movements he was past her, the puck still on his stick.

Travis had never seen anything like it. Was this how the twelve-year-olds in Brantford felt when they realized they were up against Wayne Gretzky? Was this what it was like to play against a young Mario Lemieux or a Jaromir Jagr?

Wiz still had the puck. He looked up and threw a quick, hard pass towards the net that his winger, swooping in from Travis's side, barely ticked with his stick.

Barely, but enough. The puck skipped once and dived in under Jenny's outstretched pad.

Aussies 6, Owls 5.

The roar of the crowd was so loud, Travis looked straight up, half convinced the roof was crashing down.

He checked the clock.

Thirty seconds. Probably not enough.

Sarah led their line over to the bench, but Muck held out his hand to stop them. He wanted them on for the final shift. Their best chance was with Sarah up front and Nish back. If they couldn't make something happen, no one could.

Sarah took the faceoff. She seemed furious that Wiz had so dazzled her moments before. She held the puck, stickhandled deftly around him, turned back and did it again, just for good measure, and then sent a pass back to Nish.

Nish surveyed the ice.

Twenty seconds left.

He began moving slowly up across centre. He saw Travis and flipped a quick pass.

Travis faked to go to centre ice, then turned sharply, heading down the boards.

The Aussie defenceman followed, aiming a shoulder at him.

Travis bounced ahead, the hard check missing him as the defender crashed into the boards.

Travis heard the crowd gasp.

He stopped, stickhandling. He sent the puck around the boards to Dmitri on the far side, and Dmitri clipped it back hard to Nish.

Ten seconds.

Nish moved in.

Wiz dove to block the shot.

Nish faked, danced around a spinning Wiz, aimed, and fired hard and high.

Ping! Off the crossbar!

Travis watched helplessly as the puck popped high in the air, turning over and over and over.

Sarah was already back of the net.

The puck landed and she scooped it, plucked

it off the ice like an NHLer, and was about to hand it back to the referee.

But no whistle had gone!

Three seconds.

Sarah, balancing the puck on the blade of her stick, stepped around the corner of the net and had her feet taken out from under her by a sliding defenceman.

But not before she whipped the puck, lacrosse-style, high into the far corner.

The referee's whistle blew! The horn went!

Owls 6, Aussies 6.

Sarah had tied the game with the Wizard's own move!

Travis's gloves and stick were already in the air. He, too, was flying, sailing towards a mound of Owls that already included Dmitri and Nish, with Sarah on the bottom.

Nish's cage was almost locked on Sarah's, Nish's face crimson as he screamed.

"YESSSSSS! SARAH!"

"Back off, Dragon Breath!" Sarah shouted, laughing. "Before I gag!"

But no one paid any attention. More bodies arrived. The bench had emptied. Travis, twisting happily in the pile, could make out Mr. Dillinger's pant leg, then Muck's jacket sleeve, then smell Muck as the big coach himself landed smack in the middle of the pile.

23

THERE WOULD BE NO OVERTIME. A TIE, THE organizers, the coaches, the managers, even the players, all agreed was the perfect ending to the perfect tournament. Aussie All-Stars 6, Screech Owls 6. Screech Owls 6, Aussie All-Stars 6. No matter how you said it, it sounded perfect.

The players lined up and congratulated each other. The Wiz had a special rap across the shins for Nish, a headlock for smaller Travis, and a bear hug for Sarah. The two of them, Wiz and Sarah, then moved off to stand together for the closing ceremonies. Travis wasn't close enough to tell for certain, but he could have sworn that Sarah was somehow smiling and crying at the same time.

There was one more order of business: the Game Star.

"It's me," Nish hissed into Travis's ear as they stood waiting for the announcement.

"How do you know?" Travis asked, thinking that Muck might have tipped him off.

"Who else?" Nish said.

Travis winced and shook his head. Nish was back to normal.

"*The* MVP *of the Oz Invitational*," the announcer's voice droned over the loudspeakers.

He paused for effect, no one daring to say a word.

"*From the Screech Owls* — WAYNE NISHIKAWA!"

The arena erupted in thunderous applause. The players banged their sticks on the ice. Nish, acting as if this were an everyday experience for him, piled his stick and gloves and helmet in Travis's arms and skated off to accept his due.

Travis watched in amazement as Nish bowed to the fans and then shook hands with the organizers.

A man in a suit pulled an envelope out of his pocket and made a big display out of handing it over to Nish, who took it and stared at it. There was no announcement over the public address as to what it was.

With the man's encouragement, Nish opened the envelope and removed a piece of paper from inside.

What is it? Travis wondered. *A cheque?*

The man, beaming, reached out to shake Nish's hand. Nish must have been stunned by the amount of money, for he dropped the paper and another organizer had to pick it up for him. The first man reached out, took Nish's limp hand, shook it hard, and slapped him on the back.

Nish turned, his mouth a perfect circle, the blood draining from his face.

He skated, weakly, back to Travis while the sticks continued rapping and the rink maintained its loud standing ovation.

"*What is it?*" Travis shouted over the cheering.

Nish said nothing. He merely handed his award over.

Travis looked at his friend. Nish was white now, his eyes half shut.

Travis unfolded the paper and read: "Free Admission for One – Sydney Harbour Bridge Climb."

The Coathanger!

Nish's mouth twisted in search of words.

Finally he found them, speaking in a voice so low Travis could barely hear.

"I think I'm gonna hurl."

THE END

THE NEXT BOOK IN THE SCREECH OWLS SERIES

Power Play in Washington

The Screech Owls are in Washington, D.C., for the International Goodwill Peewee Championship – and Nish is about to become a "news flash" seen round the world! Literally. Because the craziest Owl ever has a brand-new plan: to streak the White House.

His way into the White House, he believes, is through the Screech Owls' new friend, who not only plays centre for the Washington Wall, but just happens to be the son of the president of the United States!

It is a hockey tournament with a difference: secret-service agents, sniffer dogs, metal detectors, world-wide media attention – and the most cunning political assassination plan in modern history.

When the Owls head for a "normal" kids' day out with their new friend, the president's son, they have no idea they are about to get involved in a dangerous international power play.

With murder the real game plan of their opponents.

Power Play in Washington *will be published by McClelland & Stewart in the fall of 2001.*

THE SCREECH OWLS SERIES